DESPERATE CHALLENGE

It was the stolofs that were the heart of Trawn's power. Neena had said so many times. The more Blade saw, the more he believed her. The great spider-creatures, the regular green ones and the golden ones from the royal stables, were monstrous and deadly machines. Anyone who stayed to fight was almost certainly doomed. The eyes were vulnerable, so were the uppermost joints of the legs, and so was a small spot under the belly. Otherwise every square inch of a stolof was covered with the scales and plates of armor that would turn the sharpest sword blade or spear point in Gleor.

"Warriors of Draad have slain stolofs in battle," Neena had said. "But only a few, and not all of those have lived through their victories. Stolofs alone would be formidable, but we could learn to meet them. The men of Trawn alone would give us a stout fight, for they greatly outnumber us, and few of our own warriors are your equal. Together, the stolofs and the warriors of Trawn may some day rule all of Gleor." Her face clouded and her eyes closed in pain as she said that.

So Blade knew that he would fight Draad's battles if he ever had a chance. He also knew that he would never have that chance unless he and Neena found a way out of the city. His fate and hers hung, if not quite by a thread, at least by a rope.

The Blade Series:

HEROIC FANTASY SERIES
22

BLADE
THE FORESTS OF GLEOR
by Jeffrey Lord

PINNACLE BOOKS   NEW YORK CITY

BLADE #22: THE FORESTS OF GLEOR

Copyright © 1976 by Lyle Kenyon Engel

An original Pinnacle Books edition, published for the first time anywhere.

ISBN: 0-523-00993-3

First printing, January 1977

Cover illustration by Ken Kelly

Printed in the United States of America

PINNACLE BOOKS, INC.
275 Madison Avenue
New York, N.Y. 10016

The Forests of Gleor

before the eyes were on him.

He would have never made it. The others Hoe would rather go down in shock overhead, but in any event as you never saw. He could hear the machine of the machine. He does not had passed the word of a moment. These machines would sway through the being of either

Chapter 1

If Richard Blade's MG hadn't burned out a bearing in Windsor, he wouldn't have been in the train wreck. He might still have been involved in an accident on the way to London, of course. The sleet storm that made the rails so slick made the roads even worse. He might have gone off the road and broken his neck, or gone into the Thames and drowned. But those would have been more private accidents.

The commuter train rattled toward London at full speed. Blade stretched his long legs out as far as he could and opened his copy of the *Times*. In the opposite seat of the compartment sat a young mother and her little girl.

Perhaps it was time he admitted that the old MG had come to the end of its road. It would be hard parting with the car after all these years of driving it. Yet he had to face the fact that the MG was no longer reliable transportation. A sentimental relic, yes. A valuable antique, too. The car hadn't been brand-new even when he bought it, and that had been when he was fresh out of Oxford. Perhaps he could find some antique-car lover to give the MG a good—

The train jerked savagely, as if it had been caught in an explosion. Blade flew out of his seat, to crash into the opposite side of the compartment. Twisting his body in midair, he just missed landing on top of the mother and child. He didn't miss the lamp fixture. The glass globe shattered and for a moment Blade felt as though his head would shatter too. Pain exploded in his skull, with a roar that for a moment drowned out the screeching of tearing, twisting metal.

1

When Blade could see and hear clearly again, he realized that the car was now tipped sharply forward. Blade unfolded himself cautiously. His head still throbbed, but otherwise there didn't seem to be anything wrong with him.

That was good. Blade had been on his way back to London when the MG gave out. In London he would sit down in a room carved out of the rock far below the Tower of London. His brain would be electronically linked to the giant computer that filled most of the room. Then the computer's inventor Lord Leighton would pull a red switch and the pulses from that computer would flow into Blade's brain. The room, the computer, Lord Leighton, everything Blade saw with his normal senses would vanish. He would whirl off into nothingness, and awake somewhere in the vast unknown they called Dimension X.

Blade was the only living human being who could travel into Dimension X and return alive and sane. He was about the most perfect combination of physical and mental qualities anyone could imagine—as long as he was in good health. If he succeeded in getting himself thoroughly battered and banged about in an ordinary train wreck, the trip to Dimension X would be off until he was fully recovered. Even Lord Leighton would have to admit that, though he would do so with the worst possible grace. Lord Leighton had the finest scientific mind in Britain and one of the worst tempers in the world.

There was also the man called J. He was one of the greatest of living spymasters, the head of the secret intelligence agency MI6, the man who saw Blade's promise while the younger man was still at Oxford. Under J's guidance Blade became one of the top agents for MI6. But to J he was also the son the older man had never had. J would be worried about Blade's accident, even though his worrying would be hidden from everyone—except Blade—behind a sober, reserved mask.

All that was for tomorrow. For the moment, Blade's job was doing what he could for the other passengers on the wrecked train. The mother and her little girl were stiff

2

with fright, but Blade couldn't see any visible injuries. Then the child opened her mouth and started bawling lustily. Blade could hardly believe any child able to make that much noise could be seriously hurt. The mother's eyes met his and she smiled sheepishly.

Blade nodded. "If you'll be all right for a bit, I'll go see about some of the others." Not everyone in the train had come through the crash as well as he and the woman and child had done. He could clearly hear screams of pain from elsewhere in the car.

The compartment's door into the corridor was jammed. "Turn your face away," Blade said to the woman. Then he braced himself and kicked hard with both feet against the door handle. Metal screeched again, the last of the glass fell out of the door, and it slid open with a crash. Blade crawled over to the doorway and looked up and down the nearly vertical corridor.

The windows on the opposite side of the corridor were all smashed, and gusts of chill damp wind blew in. At the bottom of the corridor several bodies were piled, covered with shattered glass. In the darkness Blade at first thought they were all unconscious or dead. Then one of the bodies groaned and sat up. The groan turned into a gasp of pain.

Blade clambered down the length of the upended car, using both hands and feet with practiced ability. As he reached the bottom, a man sat up. He looked about thirty, and one arm dangled uselessly.

"Can you get up?" said Blade. There was a certain risk in moving the man. He might have internal injuries. But there was no way to get at the people under him without his moving.

"I—I suppose so," said the man.

"Come on, I'll help you up." Blade took the man by his good arm and shoulder. The man gritted his teeth and rose to his feet with another gasp. Blade braced himself and supported the man until he was steady on his feet. Then the man clambered painfully out through the nearest window, pulling with his good arm as Blade pushed from below. He dropped to the ground with a

3

loud yelp of pain, then Blade heard him getting to his feet.

"All right?"

"I think so," came back from outside.

"Good. Help's going to be along pretty soon, so don't wander off. If you have to move, watch out for fallen wires."

"All right."

Blade turned to the next victim. This was an older woman, well dressed, unconscious, and with a trickle of blood from one corner of her mouth. Moving her would definitely be too risky. But there was a third person down there, visible under her feet.

Blade gently lifted the woman's feet and saw a small boy held upright among the twisted metal plates. Blade saw no blood, but a twisted length of steel bar was pressing into the boy's back, trapping him in the wreckage. Blade bent down, discovered that he could just reach the bar, and took a firm grip on it with both hands. Then slowly he heaved.

Blade stood more than six feet tall and weighed two hundred and ten pounds. He had both enormous strength and great experience in using that strength. He needed all of both to pull the bar away from the boy. A fraction of an inch at a time, the bar gave, as sweat popped out on Blade's forehead, as sharp stabs of pain flared in arms and shoulders and chest, as his shirt split down the back with a sharp ripping sound that he barely noticed. Then the space was wide enough for the boy's shoulders. Blade put one hand under each of the boy's arms and lifted slowly. Easily and effortlessly, the boy rose to freedom.

Blade lifted the boy in both arms and carried him outside. He laid him on the damp grass, made sure he was still breathing normally, then returned to the car.

There might be other people, trapped still farther down in the twisted metal of the car's forward end. If there were, they were either dead or beyond Blade's helping. He clambered back up the dark corridor, looking into each compartment for people he could help. He found them.

4

An older man, sprawled helplessly and apparently choking to death. Blade bent over him and used mouth-to-mouth breathing until the choking stopped and the thin chest began to rise and fall normally. Then he pulled a blanket from the rack overhead and spread it over the man.

A woman, slowly bleeding to death from glass cuts in her leg, while the other three people in the compartment stared helplessly at her face going white. Blade pulled the woman's silk scarf off her head and used it as a tourniquet. "Now—one of you loosen that scarf every ten minutes once the bleeding stops. Understand?"

Vague nods. Blade knew the others were still in shock, but he had to hope for the best. He scrambled out and on upward.

Sometimes there were people who were beyond help— an old woman who lay with her head twisted at an impossible angle and no pulse at all in her bony wrist. As Blade searched for the pulse that wasn't there, a small boy tugged at the woman's other hand.

"Grandma, grandma, wake up! I'm scared!"

Blade had to get out of that compartment quickly.

In other compartments there were people who needed nothing but a little time to recover from the shock of the accident. One of them had the sense to hand Blade a large flask filled with brandy. He passed it around.

"Don't try climbing out unless you feel in the pink," he said. "It would be bloody silly to fall down the corridor and break your necks *now*." The remark drew nervous laughter. "Don't try moving any of the injured, either. We don't know how they're hurt." They nodded and Blade moved on.

Pick glass out of wounds, wad handkerchiefs over gashes and cuts, apply tourniquets, use mouth-to-mouth respiration, give sips of brandy and words of encouragement—everything blended together in a single swirling chaotic nightmare until Blade no longer remembered details. He didn't care about that. What he did care about was keeping going until there were no more people in the

5

car to look at. Then he would start on the next car, and then on the last, and then—

He'd just reached the rear of the car when the sound of approaching sirens and motorcycle engines reached his ears. A red flashing light glowed through the storm, then a yellow one.

Blade suddenly realized that he had to get out of here. He'd done what he saw as simple duty. But the police and the papers would still call him a hero. He would be standing in the full spotlight of publicity for days or even weeks.

Blade had a cover identity, of course. But could it defend him from all the questions the papers and the BBC would be asking? Even more important, could it defend every bit of the secret of Project Dimension X? Blade wondered.

Well, he'd done his duty in one way. Now he had to do it in another. He had lived in the shadows ever since he joined MI6. It was time to slip away into those shadows again.

Blade scrambled across to a window, kicked a few jagged pieces of glass out of the frame, and dropped to the ground. He landed heavily on hands and knees, but rose quickly to his feet. He was gone into the storm before the first motorcycle pulled up beside the wrecked train.

It was another hour before the chief constable for the county appeared. By that time the doctors had finished sorting the hundred-odd passengers into the dead, the hurt, and the unharmed. The three derailed cars and the smashed locomotive still sprawled hideously across the landscape. In the gloom and the falling sleet, the emergency lights made the cars look grotesquely twisted and bloated.

The chief constable's irritation at being dragged out of bed in such grisly weather vanished in a moment. He hadn't seen anything this bad since the Blitz!

"Good God! What happened?"

The police inspector in charge shook his head. "The

6

Railway people think it may have been ice on the tracks, so that they hit this curve too fast. But that's only a guess."

"How many—?"

"Twelve so far, and about forty hurt. We've also got a bit of a mystery on our hands."

"Oh? How so?"

"It seems there was this chap who went clambering around one car like a ruddy monkey, giving first-aid to everyone. The doctors say he saved a good half-dozen lives. But he's nowhere around now."

"Did you get a good description of him?"

"Oh, certainly, sir. Big fellow, over six feet, and heavily built. Dark hair and skin, but dressed like—well, like a gentleman. A good dozen people would probably be able to recognize him."

The chief constable nodded, considering the mystery. Dash it all, he didn't want to track down a man who'd apparently been more than a bit of a hero, and who might have some perfectly good reason for disappearing after he'd done his work! But there was no doubt about it—the mystery man's behavior was suspicious, and part of the chief constable's job was to follow through on his suspicions.

"Well, I think we'd better get out a 'wanted for questioning' bulletin on this fellow. Also, ring up the Yard and see about having an artist sent out. With a dozen good witnesses we should be able to get a fair enough composite drawing of him."

"Yes sir."

Chapter 2

At about the same moment, Blade was on the telephone in a small pub about three miles away. He was talking to J. If the chief constable could have overheard Blade's end of the conversation, it might have set his mind at rest

7

about Blade's being a criminal. It would still have left him wondering just exactly who Blade was.

"—no indication of anyone coming after me, at least not yet. I've told the pubkeeper that I had a bit of a car accident. Yes, he's heard of the train wreck. But the rumor going around is that everybody aboard was either killed or so badly hurt they won't be running around the countryside. He believes my story, at least so far.

"Fingerprints? Yes, of course. But I threw the brandy flask into a ditch. If they find it and recognize it, I doubt if it will show a recognizable print. No, not at all, sir. I appreciate your wanting to cover every point.

"Official car? By all means. Traffic on the line will be snarled for hours, and a car could be out here before I could find a bus or cab. The Red Bull, Ackerbury. Yes, it's the only Red Bull in town. About an hour and a half. Good. Thank you, sir, and see you Wednesday morning."

Blade hung up. The pubkeeper was looking at him sympathetically. "Bit of a bother, the old bus giving out, wasn't it, guv'nor?" He hesitated. "Me brother Al runs a bit of a garage over t'west of town. I could give him a call and—"

Blade shook his head. "Thanks, old man, but Al can sleep in peace tonight. Nothing's going to help my car now, and I've already done what's necessary with the police. So if you'll just draw me another pint, I'll keep out of your way until my ride arrives."

"Anything you say, guv'nor." The beer tap hissed.

Thirty miles away, in a flat in the West End of London, the man called J also hung up his telephone. He leaned back in the leather armchair and lit up a cigar. That was one over the limit his doctor allowed him now, but damn the limit and damn the doctor! Compared to the risks Richard Blade took week in and week out, an extra cigar was nothing.

There was something grimly ludicrous about this new situation. Here was Richard, reacting superbly in a crisis, as he naturally would. In fact he had reacted so superbly that he had quite accidentally made himself a first-class

8

hero. Never mind his modest account of the affair. From long experience J could usually guess what lay behind Richard's modest accounts. Probably a dozen people at least owed him life or limb.

Yet there was *no bloody way* Richard could ever get the credit he deserved! J almost shouted the words aloud in his frustration. Richard had done exactly the right thing in slipping away quietly. But it was a damned shame that had to be the right thing to do!

Well, Richard was a professional and a gentleman. He would not cry over the inevitable. But one of these days, J swore, he would do *something* to see Richard get some part of the credit he deserved for all he had done for England. Someday, somehow, if it was the last thing he did.

By the time J reached that thought, he had also reached the end of his cigar. Since he couldn't think of anything else that needed his attention that night, he went to bed.

Blade appeared at the Tower of London promptly at ten o'clock Wednesday morning. To J's eyes he showed no sign of as much as a shaving-nick, let alone having been in a train wreck.

"I gather the doctor gave you a clean bill of health?" said J.

"Absolutely, sir," replied Blade. "He couldn't find anything except a bit of bruising on the scalp."

"What about the X-rays?"

"Nothing showed up on those either. It seems I still have the same old hard head."

"That's good. It would be a trifle on the silly side to have you survive twenty-odd trips and then buy it in a train wreck here in England."

"I quite agree." J's words were a monumental under-statement. For all his qualities of mind and body, Blade also knew that he was still alive partly because of good luck that could run out at any time. It certainly *would* be bloody silly to have it run out here in England, when he spent so much time in so much danger in Dimension X.

Blade reached up to press the elevator button. "I see

9

you're wearing a ring," said J, looking at the raised hand. "Ruby?"

"Yes. Nothing really fancy, though. My father gave it to me when I left Eton."

"Are you going to try wearing it into Dimension X?"

Blade recognized the concern in J's voice. The older man didn't care very much for anything that increased the uncertainty of Blade's trips into Dimension X. Blade didn't blame him, particularly after the last trip.

It wasn't quite correct to say that everything had gone *wrong* the last time, but certainly a lot hadn't gone the way it was planned. Blade had ended up being bounced about from one dimension to another, first with a courtesan from the black-jade city of Kano, then with a Russian secret agent Lord Leighton had sent into Dimension X as a way of disposing of her. It had been nearly the hairiest mission in the whole history of Project Dimension X, and that was saying a good deal.

"Yes, sir, I am. It's small and light, so it won't take up any room or throw me off balance. Also, it's something that's been around me for quite a while. If there *are* such things as a human body's individual—oh, call them 'vibrations'—it's more likely to be 'in tune' with mine than something like a survival pack or even a survival knife."

J frowned. "Sounds rather like mystical guesswork to me."

Blade shrugged. "It could be mystical, and I'll admit it's guesswork. But isn't half the whole Project guesswork?"

J had to laugh. "You're perfectly right. Only don't let Lord Leighton hear you say that. The man will never forgive you," he added drily, "Ah, here's the elevator."

The elevator took them two hundred feet below the Tower in a few seconds. Then they walked down a long corridor, passing through a series of electronically monitored security doors to the main computer complex.

The outer rooms of the complex were filled with the supporting equipment and technicians for the main computer. There seemed to be more of both each time Blade came through.

One face was missing from among the technicians, though. Katerina Shumilova, computer technician and crack KGB agent, lay dead in Kano, killed defending the city against the attacks of the fierce Raufi from the desert. Katerina Shumilova, technician, enemy agent, and a woman Blade had loved. This was the only place in Home Dimension that could really remind Blade of her, and perhaps that was just as well. He could and would fight off all his memories of her, but he would be happier not to have to do so very often.

Another, more familiar face peered around the last door at them as they approached it. Lord Leighton was already at work in his private sanctum, the room that housed the main computer. He waved Blade and J on in through the door. Silently it slid shut behind them.

Leighton noticed Blade's ring almost at once. The man was past eighty, his legs twisted by polio, his spine distorted by a hunchback, what little remained of his hair milky white, and his lab coat as rumpled and dirty as an unwashed dish towel. There was nothing wrong with his eyes, however. They missed very little.

Somehow the ring did not touch off an explosion of Leighton's famous temper. Blade had been half-expecting one. The scientist's ego was as great as his genius. He usually took a dim view of anybody else adding to *his* experiments.

Instead, all that he said was, "You've thought it out, I take it?"

Blade nodded, and repeated what he'd told J. Leighton listened almost politely—another surprise!—then nodded slowly.

"All this seems compatible with my own data. Certainly if there are any incompatabilities, we can't expect to discover them without going ahead. Very well. Wear the ring, and good luck with it."

J went over to the folding observer's chair, pulled it out of the wall, and sat down. Blade headed for the little

11

changing room carved out of the solid rock of the walls of the computer room.

As he stripped off his clothes, he wondered why Lord Leighton was behaving in such a subdued fashion. It might be simple old age at long last catching up with him, but that was hard to believe. Perhaps Leighton simply felt a little less unsure of himself than before. All the accidents of Blade's last trip had proved beyond any doubt how little anybody really knew about Dimension X, or what went into sending a person there and bringing him back. For all his egotism, Lord Leighton was too honest a man and too good a scientist not to admit ignorance when it was so dramatically demonstrated—or when it would endanger Richard Blade. Blade doubted he'd ever really like the scientist the way he liked J. But certainly he was coming to respect the old boffin more with each crisis.

Blade finished stripping himself, then smeared every inch of skin with a greasy black cream. It smelled dreadful, but it was supposed to prevent electrical burns when Blade was wired into the computer. Perhaps it actually did. Then he stepped out of the changing room, wearing only the grease, the ruby ring, and a small loincloth.

He walked over to the glass booth in the center of the room and sat down in the metal chair inside the booth. The rubber seat of the chair felt chill and slick, almost slimy against his skin. He leaned back and let Lord Leighton go to work.

Lord Leighton bustled about, unwinding long wires in a dozen different colors from the towering, crackle-finished gray consoles of the computer. Each wire ended in a gleaming metal electrode, shaped like a cobra's head. Swiftly but as carefully as a brain surgeon, Leighton taped the electrodes to Blade's skin, one after another, until Blade was covered with them from head to foot. They even hung from his earlobes, his toes, and his penis.

Eventually there were no more electrodes or at least no more places to attach them. Lord Leighton backed away from Blade's chair. Blade felt like raising a hand in salute to the scientist. But he was so completely covered with

12

electrodes and wires that he hardly dared even take a deep breath.

By now the computer was through the preliminary phases of the main sequence. It was time for Lord Leighton to take over, as he always did, for the moment that would send the computer's pulses into Blade's brain, twisting his perceptions, twisting and hurling him out of the chair and the room and London, into Dimension X.

Blade sometimes felt like twitting Lord Leighton about his insistence on manually controlling the huge computer. Did the scientist harbor secret doubts about the computer that was the product of his own genius?

Hardly. All Leighton was doing was *not* assuming that the computer was completely infallible, and playing human backup at the decisive moment. Blade knew perfectly well the limitations of automatic systems without human backups. He'd outwitted far too many of them as a field agent for MI6. Lord Leighton would have been a fool not to take a hand. No one, not even his worst enemies, had ever called him a fool, or ever would.

Leighton stepped up to the master control panel and scanned the lights playing across it. His hand came to rest lightly on the red master switch. Blade's eyes swung toward the switch and focused on it and the long thin hand above it. He saw J do the same.

Then the hand came down on the switch, the switch slid down in its slot, and Blade's world fell apart.

Every bit of the room shook and vibrated wildly, with a tremendous deafening roar. Wild lights in a dozen nightmarish eye-searing colors flashed and flared and ran up and down the walls, across the floor, around the booth.

Cold blue fire played around Blade, long flames jetting out and sparks trailing from his fingers and toes, the tips of his ears and nose, even from his penis.

The roar grew louder. Suddenly a giant spring seemed to uncoil beneath the chair and the booth, hurling them upward. Blade braced himself to be smashed to jelly against the rocky ceiling of the room. The rock seemed to melt away from the blue fire, like piles of sand washed

13

away by an incoming wave. Blade roared up through the rock and into the gray daylight of London.

He climbed higher and the Tower of London dropped away below him, shrinking until it looked no larger than a model he'd played with as a child. In all directions London spread out below him. He could make out the dull gleam of the Thames, the spires of Westminster Abbey and the Houses of Parliament, the dome of Saint Paul's, the haze from factories farther out in the suburbs and farther down the river.

Still higher. Now the horizon began to curve, and he felt the cold of the stratosphere biting at his fingers and toes like a swarm of icy teeth. Somehow he felt no dizziness, no fading of vision, nothing to suggest that he was short of oxygen even in the thin air around him. It was as if the glass booth was a capsule that kept in the air but could not keep out the cold.

Higher still. He had seen a satellite picture of London once. The scene below was beginning to remind him of that picture. He could not be a hundred miles high over southeastern England, but he was seeing everything that he could have seen from up there. The part of his mind that was still capable of analysis told him that this was a new kind of twisting of his senses by the computer.

That moment of analysis seemed to trigger something in Blade's mind. With horrible suddenness all the remaining sensations of being naked a hundred miles above the earth crashed in on him. The cold was a flaming agony in every part of his body, until he wanted to shout out loud. He saw his skin turn snow white, as his sweat turned to ice crystals in a second.

He wanted to shout, but he couldn't. All the breath in his body was exploding out of his lungs. His blood was not freezing, but it was boiling. He felt heart and veins and arteries rupturing, felt pink foam bubbling up inside of him and saw it spew out of his mouth. The pink foam poured out, formed a great cloud around him, blotted out the star-filled blackness above and the earth below. As his

14

vision faded, so did all his other senses, until at last Richard Blade felt nothing at all and died alone in his chair high above the earth.

Chapter 3

Blade slowly drifted back to consciousness. He felt warm breezes on his skin, long damp grass under him, heard the rippling of water. He also felt his head pounding like a furiously beaten drum. He lay quietly until the pounding began to fade away.

He felt surprised at being alive. The sensations of rising high above the Earth and then freezing and exploding in a vacuum had been much too vivid. He had never felt his own death with such gruesome realism.

But whatever he'd felt, he was still alive. He sat up and began to flex each finger and toe, each muscle of each arm and leg. He was not only alive, but apparently unhurt. As he flexed the fourth finger of his left hand, he felt a stiffness in it that wasn't a torn or bound muscle. He stared down at the finger. The ruby ring seemed to stare back at him.

Blade gave a shout of delight and sprang to his feet. He sprang up too fast for his still shaky coordination. His feet slipped on the wet grass and went out from under him. He sat down again even faster than he'd leaped up, jarring his headache into life again. He sat and turned his hand back and forth, watching the ruby glow like a hot coal as the sunlight struck it.

The ring weighed only a couple of ounces altogether, and the ruby only a couple of carats. Yet they represented something monumental and magnificent to Blade. After all the years of Project Dimension X, he had finally succeeded in bringing something from Home Dimension into Dimension X! It looked as if his guess about the ring had been right. He would certainly have something to tell Lord Leighton when he got back.

15

Blade realized that the headache was fading away again. Or perhaps he was just feeling too happy and triumphant about the ring to notice minor discomforts. One small ruby ring wasn't a survival kit, or a rifle, or even shorts and a pair of hiking boots. But it could be the start of better things. On his own, and out of his own imagination, he'd made a major breakthrough for the whole Project, and for England.

More cautiously than before, Blade rose to his feet and looked around him. He wanted to orient himself, and also find something to use as a weapon. The next time he tried to take something into Dimension X, he'd try his old commando knife. It had been around him even more than the ring, since he'd taken it on several missions for MI6. It would also be a bloody sight more useful than the ring!

Blade saw that he was standing in knee-high grass on the bank of a small river. The bank sloped downward to his left, then dropped vertically about a yard to the water. To his right the ground sloped gently upward. As the ground rose the grass gave way to clusters of bushes and small trees. Towering beyond them was a solid wall of trees that soared upward a hundred feet or more. Some of the real giants thrust their spreading, vine-tangled crowns up twice that high. The breeze blowing from the forest was warm and heavy with the odors of both growth and decay, of flowers, mold, and damp earth that had never seen the daylight.

There were no fallen branches in sight, at least none that weren't too small or too rotten to be useful. Blade walked over to a limber sapling, about six feet tall and three inches thick at the butt. Gripping it with both hands, he began bending it back and forth, putting all his strength and weight into each heave. The sapling was even tougher than he'd expected, but one by one the fibers of the wood parted. At last one tremendous heave snapped the last few, and the sapling came free in Blade's hands.

By the time he'd stripped off all the branches, he was sweating in the steamy heat and his hands were turning red and smelly with sap. He had his weapon, though. The

16

stripped-down sapling would make a very respectable quarterstaff.

That would be good enough for the moment. Blade had been active in the medieval club at Oxford. Instead of rowing or tennis, he'd worked out with mace, broadsword, and other traditional weapons, including the quarterstaff. In fact, he'd become noted for his deadly skill with the quarterstaff, a skill he'd never lost and one which had saved his life in more than one exotic dimension.

Blade tossed his staff up in the air and caught it with one hand. As always, he felt better with a weapon. Not that he was helpless with only what nature gave him—he held a fifth-*dan* black belt in karate, and there were very few of the martial arts he couldn't use in a pinch. A weapon, though, always gave him an extra line of defense or an extra method of attack. He could never be sure that wouldn't be important, and in fact it usually was.

With his staff in one hand, Blade walked down to the bank of the river. He looked around carefully, with the wariness of a prowling animal. There was nothing that looked dangerous anywhere in sight.

Holding onto a root with one hand, Blade lowered himself slowly down the yard-high embankment into the water. It cooled and refreshed, washing away sweat and the last of his headache. He cupped his free hand, then drank and drank until his throat was no longer dry. Then he gripped the root with both hands, heaved himself up the embankment, and stood on the grass again. Water dripped down off him as he bent to pick up his staff.

As he straightened up, staff in hand, he heard a shrill, sharp scream from among the bushes that lay between him and the forest. It was a woman's scream—no, two women. The screams weren't fear, though. They held surprise and anger, but no fear. Blade held his staff crosswise in both hands, then stalked toward the source of the noise.

The screams came and went quickly. Other noises followed—grunts, heavy breathing, a war cry unmistakably from a man's throat, the sound of heavy footfalls and cracking branches as a small battle exploded into action.

17

The battle was going on well in toward the forest. Blade slowed his advance. Somebody might need help, but he wouldn't be much good if he barged in blindly, taking out the wrong side or even getting taken out himself.

A sudden *whick* of something slicing fast through the air was followed by the *thunk* of something else smashing solidly into bone. The *whick-thunk* came again. This time a man screamed in pain. Blade heard the sound of heavy, lurching footsteps, two sets of them. They moved rapidly toward him, branches rustling and twigs crunching as the people staggered along.

Two men in short leather tunics and sandals burst out of the bushes. One of them hobbled and limped, favoring his left leg. The left kneecap was a smashed, bloody mess. As he emerged into the open the leg gave way entirely, and the man sat down on the grass with a whimper. A short sword dropped from his hand.

The other man staggered on, his eyes staring blindly about him. One side of his skull was cracked wide open, and blood trickled from his ears and his mouth. He clutched a short throwing spear in one hand.

The man staggered toward Blade, passing within a yard of him without showing that he knew Blade existed. Blade turned to see the man stagger on toward the river, his dying brain sending its last impulses to his legs. He reached the edge, toppled over the embankment, and vanished from sight with a splash and a gurgle.

A howl behind Blade made him spin around. The man with the smashed knee had lurched to his feet and was coming at Blade, sword raised. Blade shifted to the right and saw the man do the same, but not fast enough. One end of Blade's staff whipped out and slashed down across the back of the man's sword hand. His sword dropped to the ground again. The man didn't stop or even shake his smashed hand in pain. With his other hand he drew a knife from a sheath in his belt and raised it to throw. Again Blade shifted position faster than his opponent could and launched his own attack. The heavy end of the staff whipped over and crashed down just above the bridge of the man's nose. The thin bone smashed inward.

18

The man staggered, lurched, then went forward onto his face. By the time Blade reached him he'd stopped kicking.

Blade bent down, and with one eye on the bushes and one eye on his job stripped off the dead man's belt. Then he retrieved both the knife and the sword and stuck them in the belt.

Before Blade could take another step toward the battle, the battle came to him. Bushes crackled and crashed as though an elephant were charging through them. Seven people exploded out into the open.

Two were women, both dressed in short green leather tunics, caps, and calf-length boots. Each had a sack on her back and wielded a quarterstaff with knobbed ends in both hands. One had a spear with a red point and red feathers on the butt slung across her back. The other had a short bow.

Four of the five men were dressed and armed like the two Blade had already seen. The fifth wore an elaborate helmet of leather studded with copper plates and a leather tunic reinforced with copper bands. He carried a long two-handed sword with a slightly curved blade and a jeweled hilt, and a bow was slung across his back. At his belt swung an elaborately carved wooden baton about a foot long.

Blade had time to see all this before anyone noticed him. When they did, the battle froze for a moment. Then the helmeted man gave a sharp, wordless command, like a dog's bark. The four soldiers swung toward the women, moving in on them in a body. The leader whirled to face Blade, then charged straight at him, sword raised. Light sparked and flared from the polished metal.

Blade stood his ground. It was obvious that the leader wanted to put the new arrival down fast, then turn back to the women. Blade had to put the leader down just as fast if he wanted to help the women.

Blade didn't try a straight block with his staff. The green wood would hardly survive a slash from that heavy sword. Instead he shifted his hands toward one end of the staff and held it with the other end downward. The sword slashed down from straight overhead, struck the staff a glancing blow, and was deflected farther downward. As the man whirled his sword back up into position, Blade snapped the lower end of his staff forward. It smashed into the swordsman's unprotected groin, hard enough to make the man wince. He was a little slow with his next slash. Blade shifted his grip on his staff and drove a second thrust into the man's groin. This time the man gasped, dropped his sword, sat down on empty air, and toppled over backward onto the grass. He lay there writhing and gasping, clutching his groin with one hand and reaching for the carved baton on his belt with the other. Blade turned toward the women.

He was moments too late to save the woman with the bow. Panicking as the four men closed in on her, she dropped her staff, unslung the bow, and launched an arrow. She didn't take enough time to aim. The arrow flew low, drilling one of the attackers through the thigh. He staggered on, grappled her about the waist as she tried to draw a knife, and heaved upward. She shot up and back, coming down with her enemy on top of her, his head butting into her stomach and his hands clawing at her bare thighs under her tunic. She screamed and the other woman came running in, whirling her staff. One knobbed end smashed down on the back of the attacker's neck, crushing spine and skull. The man jerked wildly, arching and twisting, then went limp with a convulsive shudder. The other three men backed off as they saw the woman standing over her comrade, staff ready to strike if they moved any closer.

At that moment Blade heard a series of high-pitched flutings and whistlings. He turned and saw that the leader was holding the "baton" to his lips with one hand and blowing it. The "baton" was a whistle or flute of some sort.

The standing woman grimaced, with a tigerish flickering of white teeth. "He has a stolof within call," she snapped. "Quickly, stranger—finish him off while I hold these pigs away from Kubona. Then we must flee, even though I am Neena."

The woman who called herself Neena seemed to know

what was happening around her. That was more than Blade did. He decided to follow her advice. He didn't know what a stolof was, but he did know that he didn't want the fallen leader summoning help of any kind. He dropped his staff, drew sword and knife, and stepped toward the man on the ground.

As Blade approached, the man lurched to his feet, teeth clamped tightly on the whistle and still blowing it for all he was worth. His sword rose, ready to slash at Blade. Blade raised his own weapons and held them to make an X. The leader's sword whistled down and drove into the upper half of the X with a clang and a bone-jarring shock. Blade held his arms as steady as iron bars and twisted sharply, twisting the leader's sword out of his hands. Blade kicked it out of the man's reach with one foot, then pivoted and drove the other foot into the man's chest. If he hadn't been wearing the copper and leather vest, the kick would have crushed in his chest. He went down again, the whistle flying from his lips. Blade stood over him, sword and knife raised and ready to drive down into throat and groin to finish the man for good.

He never had a chance to drive home the final thrusts. The leader's whistling had done its work, and the stolof he had been calling answered the call.

Blade was suddenly conscious of a loud chittering noise in the bushes to his left, the sound of bushes being trampled, and another sound he couldn't really describe. It sounded like several large baskets being slowly crushed under the foot of some monstrous animal.

Then the bushes parted and the stolof came into view. Blade knew that this must be a stolof, and he knew that it existed. He found this hard to believe, but he had no choice when it was coming at him.

The stolof looked like a spider, but a spider four feet high and eight feet long, with a head the size of a basketball and eight legs as thick as small trees that ended in clawed feet. Three red eyes glared out of the head, and a great hideous slime-oozing grayish white sack bobbed under the monster's throat. It was covered all over with scales or sheets of something that looked like green plas-

21

tic, and it chittered and crunched as it stamped toward Blade.

It was real, it was there, and however much Blade might wish it or himself elsewhere, he could do nothing about it. Nothing, except to fight it as best he could and kill it if possible.

Chapter 4

Blade promptly dove to snatch up his staff again. He was going to need something longer than the sword to help keep the stolof at a safe distance while he figured out the best way to kill it. That green armor looked tough. Attacking the joints of the legs wouldn't help much, either, not with eight legs. The eyes looked vulnerable. He would go straight in, keeping the forelegs and mandibles busy with the staff, then thrust at the eyes. Blade shifted his staff to his left hand, drew his sword again, and moved in.

As he did, the enemy leader blew three sharp notes on his whistle. The stolof reared back on its four rear legs, thrusting out with the others toward Blade. The grayish-white sack under its throat swelled and pulsed. Then out of its mouth shot a long ribbon of something white. The ribbon arched out thirty feet and fell soggily on Blade's sword arm. He felt the stuff sticking to his skin, dropped his staff, and drew his knife to slash the ribbon apart. Before he could draw, the creature twisted sideways. The ribbon tightened so violently that Blade was jerked forward to sprawl in the grass on his face.

Blade held onto his weapons, though. As he struck the ground he slashed out at the ribbon. His knife hacked halfway through it at one stroke. But the stuff was tough. It stuck to the knife and to Blade's hand. He shook the knife furiously, then scraped it hard on the grass, trying to get rid of the clinging ribbon. It clung like glue.

Meanwhile the stolof was slowly backing away, pulling

Blade along on his stomach as it moved. Blade felt as though the hair on his arm was being pulled out by the roots and the skin pulled off the flesh.

The ribbon snapped, and he heard a cry of delight from Neena. He also heard an angry shout and more whistling from the stolof's master. Blade sprang to his feet. Before he could take a step, another ribbon shot out, this one slapping itself across his legs. The creature heaved again, and Blade went over backward.

This time the creature did not try to keep the ribbon tight. It lumbered foward, chittering and clattering and hissing like a small steam engine. Blade found that his staff was just within reach. He snatched it up and swung it one-handed at the stolof as the beast loomed over him. He aimed for one of the eyes. The staff wasn't quite long enough, and the heavy mandibles closed on it. The creature jerked back, and the staff was jerked out of Blade's hand. A moment later came the crunching of wood being pulped as the mandibles closed, chopping the staff in two. The stolof hissed again and came on.

Blade still had his sword and a grim determination to go down fighting, but not much else. He tried to rise to his feet, but the creature twisted to one side, tightening the ribbon. Blade toppled again. Once more he slashed at the ribbon, but he was jerked to one side, and the ribbon wound itself around his legs. His blow thudded down into the grass.

Before Blade could move again, the stolof deliberately bit off the ribbon and launched another one. This one fell with grisly accuracy squarely across Blade's face. His bellow of rage was stifled as the gray-white, slimy stickiness covered his mouth and nose. It felt as loathesome against his skin as the flesh of a decayed corpse, and it smelled like a combination of a poorly tended pigsty and long-overripe cheese. Blade fought down an urge to vomit. He slashed furiously but blindly at where he thought the ribbon ought to be. His sword whistled through empty air and struck one of the stolof's massive legs. It was like hitting a solid column of hard rubber. His sword struck with a dull *thunk* and bounced off. He struck again, harder.

23

This time the creature kicked out as Blade slashed. The shock was so great that Blade's sword flew out of his hands. He rolled over, clutching at the ribbon across his face with both hands, desperately trying to tear it loose before the creature was on him.

He knew he'd never make it. The stolof's hissing and chittering sounded almost overhead, and he could smell its sour, acrid odor. He could hear the clicking of the mandibles, the ones that had pulped the wood of his staff. Those mandibles would shear through his bones as if they were made of balsa wood. He heaved on the ribbon, felt it pull free—along with skin and eyelashes—felt the mandibles touch the back of his neck, and heard a sudden shout and burst of whistling behind him.

Instantly the stolof backed away from its victim. Before Blade could take advantage of that, the leader ran over to him and laid the point of his sword gently to the back of Blade's neck.

"It would be wiser not to move," said the man coldly. Blade had to agree.

The man bound Blade's hands behind his back with a length of wire twisted painfully tight, then added a thin cord. The cord seemed to be studded with tiny metal spikes that slashed and gouged Blade's skin. He could feel the blood oozing from his wrists.

Blade's ankles were already wrapped up in the stolof's ribbon. The leader left the ribbon on, but added another length of wire as a precaution. When he'd finished that, the leader jerked Blade up into a sitting position, stripped the ruby ring off his hand, and left him.

Sweat and the slime from the ribbon were oozing into Blade's eyes and blurring his vision, but he could see clearly enough what had happened to the women. The first one, Kubona, lay unconscious on the ground, her face a bloody mask. The second one, Neena, also lay on the ground. She lay face down, with two of the men kneeling on her arms and a third sitting on her legs. She must have been in considerable pain, but her face showed nothing except furious rage. She was cursing her captors quietly but continuously and in startling detail.

24

The leader went over to Neena and his men. They rose as he approached. Before Neena could move, the leader kicked her smartly in the stomach. As she doubled up, gasping and obviously trying not to vomit, the leader grabbed her by her long black hair and jerked her to her feet. Then he held her by the hair with one hand, gripped the collar of her tunic with the other, and jerked downward with all his strength. The tunic ripped apart from neck to hem and fell to the ground. Neena stood there, wearing nothing but a look of agony and grim determination. She seemed to catch her breath, then her face twisted and she spat squarely into the leader's eyes.

His face darkened and his fingers tightened in her hair. Then his other hand came up and across her face, five, ten, fifteen times in rapid succession. Each time he struck hard enough to snap her head back. Without his grip on her hair she would have fallen. When he'd finished, her face was as red as if it had been burned, and blood trickled from a split lip. Yet somehow she managed to stand, still glaring at the leader. He slapped her again, she went down, and as she sprawled on the ground he kicked her in the stomach again.

The three surviving warriors looked expectantly at Neena, than inquiringly at their leader. He shook his head.

"She's not for you. Not even for me. That is Neena of Draad, daughter to King Embor. She is fit only for *our* king. We shall bring her safely to King Furzun, and your reward will be enough to buy all the women even such as you could wish."

The faces of the three men showed a mixture of disappointment and anticipation. The leader knelt down beside the writhing Neena and drew more cord and wire out of the pouch at his belt. He blew briefly on his whistle, and the stolof drew back, folded its legs, and lay down beside some bushes. Then he pointed to Kubona. By this time she was conscious, moaning softly, and trying to sit up.

"We cannot manage three prisoners, though. That one is yours."

"We thank you, Lord Desgo," said one of the men. He

25

and the others bowed. Then they drew their knives and went to work on Kubona.

Blade had seen more ugly sights in his life than twenty ordinary men, and thought he was reasonably hardened. He still found that what the three warriors did to Neena's companion was more than he could stand. If there had been anything in his stomach, it would have come up.

After a while he found he had to close his eyes. He wished he could also close his ears. It took the woman a long time to stop screaming, because the warriors knew exactly what they were doing to her. It took her even longer to die, for the same reason. In the end Blade had to open his eyes and look at the bloody, twitching *thing* on the grass that had once been a young woman.

Blade didn't like these people. He was thoroughly nauseated by Lord Desgo and the three warriors. Compared to them, the stolof seemed almost friendly and harmless.

But these sadistic thugs were not the only people in this dimension. Somewhere else in or beyond the forests was Neena's homeland, Draad.

There was also Neena, who might not end up being thrown to King Furzun like a bone to a dog if he stayed alive to help her. Finally, there was Lord Desgo, whom he might have a better chance to kill some time in the future.

All this together meant keeping his temper and staying alive. He had plenty of good reasons, but it still wasn't going to be an easy job.

Chapter 5

A week's journey through the jungle followed. Lord Desgo was careful to keep both Blade and Neena not necessarily healthy, but alive. He made sure that they got enough food and water to keep them on their feet, and made even more sure that they had no chance to escape. Blade stayed alert, but it didn't do him much good.

He might have had a chance of escaping if he'd moved during the first three days. But Princess Neena seemed too stunned and apathetic to be able to make the escape with him. Blade wondered if the princess might be pretending to be more shaken than she really was, to lull her captors into relaxing. She'd been fierce and defiant right up to the end of the battle.

But Blade couldn't be sure. Kubona's ghastly death and her own captivity might have really unnerved the princess. He could not attempt his own escape if that would mean leaving her helpless in Lord Desgo's hands.

On the morning of the fourth day, Blade awoke to find that reinforcements had joined the party. Four more warriors and another stolof had come in during the night, to place themselves under Lord Desgo's command. The soldiers were not particularly happy about his orders to leave Neena alone, however. Blade caught them throwing numerous longing looks at her.

He could understand those looks. Battered, bruised, and dirty as she was, Princess Neena was a strikingly beautiful woman. She was long-limbed and slender, with little spare flesh anywhere, but beautifully muscled and graceful in all her movements. Her small breasts were perfectly molded, and so were all her other curves. Her hair was a gleaming black, so dark that it showed blue tints in the sunlight. Under the dirt her skin was an exquisite copper-gold. Blade could understand those lustful looks of the warriors, and why Lord Desgo expected great favor from King Furzun for giving him Neena.

The four newcomers appeared to accept Lord Desgo's authority without question, but Desgo did not trust to appearances. He was careful that the newcomers took the lead on the march. He never let any of the four get behind him, or turned his back on them. Desgo and his men always slept in a tight circle around the prisoners, one man awake and on guard at all times. Lord Desgo was obviously a warrior who thought as well as fought, and a leader his own men at least would obey and follow.

This went on for three days as they marched through the jungle. The ground underfoot was always level, and spongy with moisture and decay. Around them was always the solid mass of the jungle's vegetation. Most of it was a hundred different shades of green, relieved only by the black or brown of tree trunks, the white of fungi, and the occasional color-splashes of flowers.

Listening to the men talk, Blade discovered that this jungle-grown land was called Gleor. The city toward which they were marching, the capital of the Kingdom of Trawn, was called Trawnom-Driba—"Great City of Trawn." There lived King Furzun, most of his warrior nobles such as Desgo, the wise men who bred the stolofs for Trawn's hunts and wars, and a great many other people.

Two days' march from the city, Lord Desgo held a drinking party to celebrate the capture of Blade and Neena. The four newcomers went out into the jungle to gather kabo nuts, shaped and colored like watermelons but with a hard shell and a yellowish milk inside like coconut milk.

While the four were out of sight, Blade saw Desgo stick a dagger into the neck of his stolof and draw out a small cup full of yellowish fluid. When the four came back, Blade saw the nobleman slip the fluid into the drinking cup that was passed around. He saw the four newcomers drink deeply from the cup, while Desgo and his men skillfully pretended to drink without letting a drop of the kabo milk down their throats.

The thick darkness of the tropical night came down quickly on the jungle, and Blade fell asleep without seeing or hearing anything more. In the morning, though, he saw the results of the party. All four of the newcomers lay stretched out dead on the ground, their faces twisted with pain and turned a dark blue.

Blade wasn't particularly surprised at that. He was slightly surprised at the cool, quiet skill Lord Desgo had shown in planning and carrying out the murder. Very definitely Lord Desgo was more than simply a sadistic

28

thug. It was not at all pleasant to think about being in his power, and what that might lead to.

Lord Desgo's warriors showed no emotion at all over the four bodies. If hope of reward wouldn't keep them quiet now and forever about the murder, fear of Lord Desgo's vengeance certainly would. Blade saw no chance of persuading the warriors to betray their master, particularly when he had nothing whatever to offer them.

With only three men again, Desgo was even more careful with his prisoners. Before starting out that morning, he hobbled both of them, tying their ankles with wire from the dead men's packs. He also tied a rope around Neena's neck, so that she could be led along like a dog. Blade realized that his chances of escaping had now become slim indeed. His chances of escaping with Neena were even smaller. He could undoubtedly force Desgo to kill him, but he wasn't that desperate yet.

So Blade settled down to pretending to be a submissive, quiet prisoner. He didn't enjoy it, and he couldn't be sure if it was fooling Desgo or not. But he also knew that he was a fairly good actor. Several times he'd been good enough to save his own life. Perhaps he could do it again.

The hobbled prisoners slowed the march. It took three days and part of a fourth to cover the remaining miles to Trawnom-Driba. By noon on the fourth day, they were marching up to the city's walls.

Trawnom-Driba sprawled along the bank of a medium-sized river in a rough oval a good four miles long and half that wide. It must have held well over a hundred thousand people.

How "great" the place was, Blade was less sure. Only a handful of the largest buildings were stone or brick. The rest were wood—some of them heavily ornamented, but others only rough planks or rougher logs. Even the wall surrounding the city was made of logs peeled and driven into the earth.

Around the wall ran a narrow, water-filled ditch. It was narrow enough so that a strong man could have jumped across—if the smell rising from the scummy brown water

29

below didn't strike him dead in midair. The wall itself sagged in many places, and was overgrown almost everywhere with tangles of creepers and flowering vines. The wall and ditch together looked just about able to keep wild animals out and keep housepets in, and that was all. Blade was certain that a hundred well-armed and well-led men could get over or through the wall any time they wanted to.

Dozens of his fellow warriors and hundreds of ordinary citizens came out to welcome Lord Desgo and his prisoners. When they learned who the woman was, they cheered raucously and waved everything from swords and spears to sandals and headcloths.

Blade could understand why. Trawn and Draad had fought each other, up and down and back and forth across the forests of Gleor, for the better part of five centuries. Now Desgo was home, bringing with him the daughter of Draad's own king. It wasn't at all surprising that Lord Desgo suddenly found himself the man of the hour.

The crowd drew aside to give Desgo's party a clear path across one of the wooden drawbridges that crossed the ditch to gates in the walls. Several boys and youths scrambled up the vines growing on the logs. They started plucking flowers and throwing them down onto the planks of the bridge, to make a scented path for Lord Desgo's entry into the city.

One of the boys reached out too far toward a particularly gorgeous blossom and lost his balance. For a moment he hung on with one hand, then the vine he was holding snapped. He plunged twenty feet straight down with a wild scream, bounced off the narrow muddy bank under the wall, and dropped into the ditch. A wave of stench even more ghastly than before welled up from the ditch.

Blade heard the boy gasping and choking as he thrashed about wildly in the filthy water. Quite a number of people turned to watch. None of them made any move to help the boy. Blade felt a chill sensation inside as he looked at the people's faces. He remembered the faces of

30

the men as they raped and tortured Kubona. The people watching the drowning boy wore the same expressions of unholy joy in someone else's agony.

"Ho, people!" shouted Desgo. "We can spare little time for this now. I must pass within and put my prizes in safety." He looked around. "Has the boy a family or a master?"

Several shouts came in reply.

"Nobody, I think."

"He's an orphan."

"Nobody's ever claimed him that *I* know."

"So be it," said Desgo. "I invoke Noble's Right against the Lone." He took a spear from one of his warriors and raised it, sighting on the boy. As the boy turned on his back, Desgo hurled the spear. It drove squarely into the boy's stomach. He gave a horrible bubbling scream, then thrashed wildly for a few more seconds and sank out of sight as the water around him slowly turned red. Another few seconds, and the spreading patch of red water was all that was left of him. Even then the people went on watching, their expressions unchanged, until the red faded away. Then slowly they made way for Lord Desgo as he led his prisoners into the city.

Inside the walls Blade had even more doubts about whether Trawnom-Driba could really be called "great." The streets were mostly rutted paths, except where standing water had turned them into stinking mud. Wretched huts, shops of all sorts, larger houses with their own walls, and what looked like temples or palaces were all jammed together without logic or pattern. Pigs wandered about, rooting in the middens and garbage heaps. Occasionally they roamed over to snatch vegetables or fruit from the food shops. Blade found it rather hard to tell where the food shops left off and the garbage heaps began. He didn't blame the pigs for having the same trouble.

The more he saw of the people and what they did, the less Blade liked them. There was a small boy, about seven years old, who came out of a door holding some small animal by the tail. The animal looked like a cross between an otter and a kitten. It was writhing and twisting and

31

squeaking frantically. Beside the shop was a small fire of twigs, burning in a brick hearth. The boy swung the animal three times around his head, then let it fly. It was a good throw—the animal landed squarely in the fire. Its squeaking turned to shrill screams that slowly faded away as Blade moved on down the street.

Blade had never before in his life felt like kicking a small boy the length of a street, like a soccer ball. But he knew that if he had been free and unguarded, he would have been extremely tempted to do just that. As it was, he couldn't even clench his fists or clamp his teeth tight shut. He kept his face expressionless and his breathing regular, walked on quietly, and wondered what he would see next.

The street ended in a rough muddy square that seemed to be some sort of public assembly place. On a wooden platform in the middle of the square two men were being publicly flogged. Blade was not surprised to see that a large and cheerful crowd had gathered around to watch the sight. On the fringes of the crowd several men had set up small stands or carts, selling cakes and fruit.

The crowd broke up as people streamed over to watch Desgo pass. Blade got a clearer view of the flogging. The executioner was a barrel-chested six-footer in a loincloth. His whip had five long plaited strands, and as he swung it Blade could see the glint of metal at the end of each strand.

One of the men was dead or dying. His back was one raw gaping mass of pulped and hacked flesh. Insects swarmed over it and in several places the white of the man's spine showed through.

The other victim was hardly more than a boy. His back was less grisly to look at, and he still had the strength to scream as the whip struck him. Blade wondered what the boy had done to deserve being flogged to death. If he'd spent his childhood throwing live animals into fires, there might be a sort of rough justice in what was happening to him. Blade doubted if he was being punished for anything like that, however. Sadistic cruelty seemed to be as popular in Trawnom-Driba as beer was in London, and just as easy to come by.

The street now wound snake-like through a tangle of close-set huts. Blade couldn't help wondering how many serious fires Trawnom-Driba had each year. In a city mostly wood, a single badly tended cooking fire could burn down half of it.

They came out of the huddled buildings into another square. On the far side was the largest building Blade had seen in the city. It had its own brick wall twenty feet high, with armed warriors walking back and forth on top of it. Beyond the wall Blade could see highpeaked roofs painted in a dozen garish colors, with beam ends carved into dozens of hideously distorted human and animal masks. Even in their art the people of Trawn seemed to cultivate pain and torment.

Desgo stopped and addressed Blade and Neena.

"I bring you to your new home, slaves. Before you lies the palace of King Furzun. What welcome you will find in that home depends much on you. King Furzun has no time to waste with unruly slaves. If you displease him, he will punish you and return you to me.

"On the other hand, if you please him in all the ways King Furzun enjoys being pleased, you will live as well as a slave may until he tires of you. Then I shall take you from him and you may continue to live with me for as long as it is given for slaves to live." Blade suspected that was not very long. Life in Lord Desgo's power would hardly be worth living, in any case. But for the time being Blade knew he would continue to be as well behaved a slave as possible. Live slaves had more opportunities to escape than dead ones.

He wasn't sure Neena would see things the same way. She'd continued to be apathetic and numb all the way to the city, not even speaking when Desgo slapped her, drinking her water and eating her food in silence. She'd watched the ghastly scenes at the walls and in the streets with a face that might have been a bronze mask. Now she looked at the palace with the same bleak, resigned ex-

33

pression. Was anything going to register, or had her mind broken under the shock of captivity?

The massive gates of the palace squealed and rumbled open. A score of guards in blue leather tunics and codpieces scurried out, with drawn swords. Desgo spoke briefly to their leader, then stepped back and let them surround his prisoners. Blade and Neena found themselves being herded in through the gates. In the darkness beneath the gate towers, Blade heard more squealing and rumbling as the gates shut behind him.

Inside the walls, the palace seemed to be a labyrinth of twisting alleys and low doors that seemed to neither come from anywhere nor lead to anywhere. The only difference between the palace and the poorer neighborhoods of the city seemed to be that the palace didn't smell as bad.

Eventually the guards led Blade and Neena up to a door of solid square beams set in a featureless brick wall. To Blade's surprise it opened at a shove from the guard captain. Total blackness yawned beyond the doorway, blackness and an almost solid stench of too many things too long dead.

Before Blade could move, four of the guards grabbed him by the arms. The leader drew his sword and in two quick slashes cut through the bonds around Blade's wrists and the hobbles on his ankles. Then all four of the men holding him gave a mighty heave. Blade felt his feet leave the ground, then he was flying forward and plunging down into the darkness beyond the doorway.

Chapter 6

Blade somehow expected the darkness to be completely bottomless. Instead he struck solid ground no more than ten feet below. He wasn't braced for the shock of landing, and sprawled face down.

The ground under him was more of Trawn's universal mud, several inches deep, slimy, cold, and foul smelling.

Blade rose on his hands and knees and spat the mud out of his mouth, then stood up. Ten or twelve feet above his head, he saw a rectangle of light—the doorway through which he'd been thrown. As he watched, several figures struggled into the light. Three were guards, the fourth was Princess Neena.

The guards did not heave Neena out into the gloom like a sack of grain. Instead they took her by the hands and lowered her over the doorsill until her feet were only a few feet above the mud. Then they let go. Neena landed with a squelching noise, staggered, and would have fallen if she hadn't reeled against the wall. She seemed unhurt.

Neena pushed herself slowly away from the wall and straightened up. As she did so, the door above slammed shut with a *thunk* that echoed hollowly in the thick air of the chamber. For a moment there was total darkness around the two prisoners again, as lightless and seemingly endless as the remotest parts of outer space. Blade heard Neena give a faint whimper of fear or pain.

The blackness lasted no more than a minute. Slowly a faint light crept into the prison, driving back the darkness. It was a pale light without color or warmth, like a winter dawn. It seemed to be coming from above. Blade looked upward, and saw a faint glow creeping through a circle of holes in the ceiling at least twenty feet above his head.

Blade looked at Neena. The princess was standing a few feet from the wall, erect and motionless, her face blank and her hands at her sides. She seemed as numb as ever, making no effort to meet Blade's eyes. He sighed with frustration, then began examining their prison.

It was a simple square chamber, about forty feet on a side and dug about twelve feet into the earth. The floor and the walls up to ground level were bare earth. Above ground level were ten-foot brick walls, with a heavily timbered ceiling on top of that. The holes from which the light was coming were set in the bottom of a large wooden drum in the exact center of the ceiling. Blade suspected that there was more than light behind those holes. The light had come on so fast that someone was almost

35

certainly up there, with ears to hear and eyes to watch what went on below.

Blade lowered his eyes, scanning the walls of the prison again. This time he saw something that made him start— a wooden grating low down in the opposite wall. Behind it was blackness.

Slowly, trying to give the impression that he was wandering aimlessly, Blade drifted over toward the grating. When he'd reached it, he sneaked a quick look at the ceiling. He might—just *might*—be outside the angle of vision of any of the holes. Or he might still be visible, but not clearly enough for the observer above to realize what he was doing. It might be a foolish risk to try anything with the grating this soon. It would be an even more foolish risk to sit around doing nothing to find out what might lie in the darkness behind it.

Blade bent down and looked carefully at the grating. It must have originally been designed to open—on one side were rusted hinges. It had been sealed shut around the edges and the lock removed. Several of the bars also looked as if they had been broken out and replaced over the years.

Blade sat down in front of the grating so that his body hid what he was doing from anyone looking down from above. Slowly he pulled on each bar, testing it. He didn't try to break the bars themselves. They were made of a dark wood as heavy and nearly as tough as wrought iron. Instead he tried to loosen them from their sockets.

Bit by bit he began to feel a little play in one of the bars. He concentrated on that one, pushing and pulling with all his strength. Sweat began to stream off him, plowing lighter paths in the dark mud that covered much of his skin.

Suddenly one end of the bar popped out of its socket, with a shower of dust. Blade now had more leverage. He forced himself to work slowly and quietly, until suddenly the other end of the bar was also free. Then he heaved, and the rotted cords that bound the bar in the middle also gave.

The missing bar left a gap barely wide enough for

Blade's head, let alone his massive shoulders. But it gave him more room to work on the others. Three more bars went quickly, and there was an opening wide enough for Blade to squeeze through. He looked back across the prison chamber. Neena was now sitting down where she'd been standing. Her face was as expressionless as ever. Blade sighed and carefully pushed himself through the hole in the grating. He was bruised and sore by the time he found himself in the dark tunnel on the other side.

As his eyes slowly adjusted to the darkness, Blade saw that the tunnel was not absolutely black. Far away—so far away that it was impossible to even guess the distance—he sat two faint patches of grayish light, one above the other. Blade smiled. Perhaps there was some other explanation. But from here it looked very much as if somewhere far down the tunnel was an opening to the light and air above.

Blade crawled forward into the darkness. He held onto one of the loosened wooden bars as he moved, using it to probe the way ahead. After only a few yards he felt the floor of the tunnel sloping downward. He moved on more slowly, occasionally pausing to feel above and to either side of him. The tunnel's cross section was roughly square, about four feet on a side. The walls were plain earth, but solidly packed and surprisingly dry. This tunnel had been dug a long while back. Blade wondered how many prisoners had found their way out through it.

Gradually the mouth of the tunnel faded to a pale, dim square incredibly far behind him. The gray light ahead seemed only a little closer. All around him were darkness and the smells of earth and air that never saw the sun.

His hand came down suddenly on something hard. He drew back, then felt cautiously. It was a human rib cage. A little exploration by touch turned up skull and leg bones. He didn't feel like looking for anything more. The bones were totally fleshless, and as dry as anything could be down here. Like the tunnel, the bones had been here for a long time.

Blade crawled past the bones and on into the darkness. It was now impossible to tell what lay around him except

37

by feel. Blade moved on still more slowly, feeling his way before each movement.

It was just as well that he did. Suddenly his probing bar came down not on solid ground, but on empty air. He swept the bar completely across in front of him. He was on the edge of a wide gap in the tunnel, where the floor dropped away into—what? In the darkness, it was going to be hard to tell.

Blade got down on his stomach, wormed his way forward until he lay on the very edge of the gap, then reached out as far as he could. He swept the bar up, down, and sideways, without meeting anything but air.

Damn! The gap might be fifty feet wide. It might also end five inches beyond the end of his probing bar. There was no way to tell, and there wouldn't be any unless he could bring some light down here. But how to do that?

Perhaps he could climb down one side of the gap, across the bottom, and scramble up the other side? It would not be impossible to kick hand- and footholds in the earth, although it would take a while.

Moving as quickly as he dared, Blade scrambled back to the skeleton. He picked up one of the bones, then crawled back to the gap. He had to find out how deep it was before he risked starting a climb down into it. He held the bone out at arm's length, then let it fall.

He heard a faint whisper of air as the bone dropped down into the blackness. It fell for a long time, gradually fading away. A still longer time after that came a faint, incredibly distant thump as the bone landed. It must have fallen close to three hundred feet.

Blade swore to himself. Climbing down one side of the gap and up the other had been a good idea, in theory. It was not going to be a good one in practice, not if losing his grip meant a three-hundred-foot fall. He understood now why the tunnel was still there and so easily accessible from the prison chamber. All it was good for was a quick way of committing suicide. Blade wondered how many prisoners had done just that, and how many sets of smashed bones lay far below in the darkness.

Slowly he turned around and started crawling back

toward the chamber. So one way out was blocked. Well, there would be others to be found, or if necessary made.

As Blade crawled back toward the main chamber, he realized that something was blocking off part of the entrance to the tunnel. A disagreeable thought flashed through Blade's mind. Had the guards come in to wait for his return and punish him for his curiosity?

Blade gripped his bar more tightly and crawled onward. Gradually he saw that the light was being blocked by a human figure sitting inside the tunnel. A few yards farther on, and he recognized Princess Neena. He practically scrambled up the last stretch of tunnel, then stopped abruptly as he reached her.

Neena's face was no longer set and expressionless. She was grinning broadly, and hugging her bare knees with both arms. Her shoulders shook with silent laughter. She looked as though she had either recovered from her numbness and apathy, or slipped out of apathy into madness.

Chapter 7

Blade's surprise must have showed on his face. Neena's eyes rose to meet his. Then she could no longer keep her laughter silent. She threw her head back and howled with laughter until the tears ran down her dirty face and the echoes ran up and down the tunnel.

Finally the princess leaned back against the wall, gasping for breath, and sighed deeply. "Oh, warrior, I am sorry if I frightened you. But you looked so funny, staring at me like an ox staring at the butcher just before the axe comes down."

Blade let the unflattering description of him pass. "Well, my lady princess, do you wonder that I was deceived? You played your part with great skill."

"I had good reason to," she said bluntly. "Can you deny that?"

"No, I—"

"Then do not complain or find excuses for yourself. I intended to deceive you as well. You looked like a warrior and a man of sense, but I could not be sure you would be a friend, or even a neutral. You seem of no people I have ever seen or heard of. I could not be sure that you would not think to buy the favor of Lord Desgo by telling him of my deception. So I aimed to convince you as well as him. Do not feel small because I succeeded. You are right, I am a skilled actress."

Blade took a deep breath and then mentally counted to ten before answering Princess Neena. She might have a great many gifts, but tact wasn't among them.

"My lady princess, you acted wisely according to what you knew. I am indeed from a land and people more distant than you could hope to know of. But I am a prince in my own right among my own people, traveling to prove myself and learn of other lands. I would not have betrayed you to Lord Desgo."

"How so?" said Neena. "Are you familiar with the ways of those of Trawn? Do you know how hard it is to buy their favor?"

"No, I had never heard of Trawn before I came to Gleor." He was tempted to add that he'd never heard of Draad either. "There are such people in my homeland, however. I know perfectly well how hard it is to buy their favor, and how seldom they keep faith even when you have sold yourself to them.

"Besides, I will not sell myself to such vile people as those of Trawn even if they are willing to buy. As a prince I have some notions of honor, and as a man I have some notions of decency. I ask you to accept that."

Neena laughed, this time softly. When she spoke, her voice was quiet and the edge was gone from it.

"Warrior—Prince—what *is* your name?"

"Blade."

"Prince Blade. I accept what you've told me. You seem the sort of man of whom I can believe this. Also, I am grateful for your opening this tunnel for us. I doubt if I would have been strong enough to get through the

40

grating. Now we have a place where we can sit and talk to each other. We will not have to be silent and look dumb or dismal to fool whoever watches from above."

It was Blade's turn to laugh. "You see things very clearly, princess. Unfortunately, I hoped for more from this tunnel than it can give us."

He told her briefly of what he'd found down there in the darkness. Neena looked sober, then frowned.

"You say there is no way to find out how wide that gap may be?"

"None that I can think of," replied Blade. "I know the gap is deep enough so that anyone who falls into it will be smashed to pieces. But the width—" He shrugged.

"Well, if the thing was not wide enough to make a barrier for prisoners, they would doubtless have sealed off the tunnel entirely. Then we would be even worse off than we are."

"Perhaps," said Blade. "But I still wonder why they didn't block all access, even to the gap. It is certainly a way to a quick death, and I imagine many prisoners must be looking for such a death."

"Those of Trawn do not find it easy to understand how the minds of other people may work," explained Neena. "They do not see their own people trying to flee from cruelty—or at least not very often. They do not expect to see other people do the same."

"Not very wise, are they?" said Blade drily.

"Perhaps it is a lack of wisdom, perhaps it is their curse from the gods."

"Curse?"

"Or so our Kaireens—the Learned Ones—say. They say the gods have cursed those of Trawn with a poison in the earth under their feet. It is a poison that rises from the earth into the water they drink and the flesh and fruit they eat."

"They look healthy enough," said Blade.

"Oh, it is not a poison that twists their limbs or blinds their eyes. It poisons their very souls so that they love cruelty and pain. They cannot understand any people who do not love these evils."

41

Blade nodded, mentally translating Neena's description into more scientific language. It sounded like soil chemicals or parasites that either infected the whole population or caused enough genetic damage to produce hereditary mental disorders in the whole population.

But if this element was in the soil or water—

"How long does it take for the poison to work?" said Blade.

Neena shrugged. "No one seems to know. The people of Trawn have been like this since we in Draad have known of their existence. You fear we may be poisoned if we stay long here?"

"Yes."

"So do I. But I think we shall not be here long—at least not alive. You agree?"

Blade nodded.

"Good. Then we have little to fear from the poison, unless it works very swiftly indeed. Of course, if you do start asking the guards for a whip to flog me, I will know that it is working in you. Otherwise I shall not lose any sleep over it."

They both laughed, and Neena began to try combing out her long dark hair with her fingers. She grimaced as she worked through the mass of snags, knots, and tangles that her hair had become.

Blade watched her as she worked, noting her sure movements, the play of expression on her pixieish face, the graceful lift of her breasts. She had both wits and wit, and she had lost neither in being captured. She would be as good an ally as he could expect, and far better than he'd dared hope for.

Blade and Neena settled down to manage as comfortably as they could hope to under the circumstances. Food and water were lowered from the doorway in buckets twice a day. There was enough food to satisfy half a dozen people, and enough water to allow for some washing. Blade left most of the washing water for Neena, since a daily scrub seemed to improve her spirits.

The food was not exactly gourmet cooking. It consisted

largely of heavily spiced stews of root vegetables, with large chunks of salted meat or fish thrown in about every third meal. It made Blade thirstier than ever, but also filled him comfortably. He was sure that on this diet he could keep up his strength as long as necessary.

"That's probably the idea," was Neena's comment. "You must be kept strong to make a prime slave. Even if they do torture you to death in the end, you will last longer and make a better show if you are strong." There was no need to say why their captors were keeping *her* strong. At least once a day the guards reminded them that King Furzun liked his women strong enough to put up a fight when he took them.

No one seemed concerned about the captives' escaping, or paid any attention to what Blade had done with the grating. Still, they took as few chances as possible. They spent only a few minutes each day in the tunnel. Each time they passed through the grating, Blade pulled the loose bars roughly back into place and held them there with globs of mud. In the dim light, the grating looked almost intact.

They never left the grating and tunnel unwatched, though. Somehow they had to find out just exactly how wide that mysterious gap might be. Blade would cheerfully have promised anything to anybody in return for fifteen minutes in the tunnel with a good torch.

As Blade expected, Neena found the waiting hard. From his own years as an agent he was used to waiting, like a cat in front of the hole of a very lazy mouse. Neena, on the other hand, was a royal lady, proud and impatient as a thoroughbred race horse. Several times a day she would spring up and stride around and around the prison like a caged tiger, until sheer exhaustion brought her to a stop.

Blade himself soon began to wonder how much longer they would have to wait. From the number of meals served, they'd already been here over a week. Lord Desgo seemed to have forgotten their existence, and as for King Furzun, it seemed that he had never even heard of them.

43

Chapter 8

"Blade, Blade—wake up."

Neena's voice cut into Blade's sleep. He struggled awake, rolled over, and sat up.

"What—?" he grunted, as he drove the fog of sleep out of his mind. Neena only pointed at the grating and the tunnel beyond it. Suddenly Blade was not only awake but alert, and he saw what Neena meant.

Far down inside the tunnel was a flickering orange glow. Wherever it was and whatever it was, it was bright enough so that the bars of the grating threw shadows on the floor of the prison chamber. That glow must be illuminating the entire inside of the tunnel. Blade got down on hands and knees, and scrambled quickly and quietly toward the grating.

A few quick jerks, and the way was open. Blade crawled through, Neena following him. In the tunnel they rose to a crouch and headed downward as fast as they could. The orange glow grew stronger as they moved.

They came to the gap. The glow showed it clearly, and the tunnel beyond. The actual source of the light lay well beyond the gap, about where Blade had seen gray daylight trickling through. Now an enormous fire was burning above, flooding the tunnel with its glow. Blade could hear the distant roar and crackle of the flames and feel puffs and waves of warm air on his skin.

Blade turned his attention to the gap that yawned at his feet, and plunged away into the depths. The blackness in the shaft below swallowed even the fire's glow after a few yards.

The width, on the other hand—Blade looked, and cursed. The far side of the gap was just under twenty-five feet away.

Damn, damn, damn—damn ten times over! A yard less, and Blade would have gladly attempted the leap. The

44

earth on both edges was firm, and there was plenty of room overhead.

As it was, the gap was just a little too wide for him to have more than a slim chance of making it safely. A chance much too slim to be worth risking, when the price of failure was a three-hundred foot plunge to certain death in the musty darkness far below.

As he'd suspected, the tunnel wasn't going to be a very good escape route. As a hiding place for moments of privacy, it was fine. As a route to a quick and merciful death it was even better. But for the moment Blade's mind was more on escaping. He suspected Neena's was the same.

He noticed that she was staring out across the gap, apparently measuring it with her eyes. Then she turned to him.

"Blade. Can you leap that?"

Blade slowly shook his head. "Not with much hope of landing safely."

She nodded. "Neither could I. But if you—well, *threw* me just as I leaped—" Again she measured the distance with her eyes. "I am light, and you look very strong. I think it could be done."

Blade frowned. "But then?"

"If we had a rope and a stake, I could push the stake into the dirt and tie the rope to it. Then I could throw the other end of the rope back to you, and you could swing across and climb out on the other side."

That seemed perfectly logical and sensible to Blade. Except—

"One of the bars from the grating will do for the stake. As for the rope—" She smiled and shook her head. "There I admit we have a problem." She pulled out a few strands of her dark hair and looked at them, then dropped them into the shaft and watched them as they floated down out of sight. "No, that will not do. Not even if I made myself as bald as a koba nut could I make a proper rope of my hair."

There was undoubtedly plenty of stout rope in Trawn. But all of it was outside their prison chamber. Damn again!

45

Neena looked at Blade, saw the sober expression on his bearded face, and misunderstood what was on his mind. "Blade—do not think that I would ask you to help me escape if there was no way out for you. I am of the royal house of Draad, and unlike those of Trawn we have some knowledge of honor. We shall escape together, you and I, or not escape at all." She rose on tiptoe and kissed him on the mouth. It was a long, lingering, warm kiss, that promised an even warmer passion at another time and place. Blade put his arms around the princess and they stood there, locked together, for some time.

As they crawled back up the tunnel, Blade was certain that Neena had made a promise she would keep. Still, if only one of them could have a chance to escape, he would make sure that it was she. King Furzun and Lord Desgo and all the stolofs in Trawn put together could do nothing worse to him than kill him. They could do a good deal more to Neena. She deserved every chance to escape that luck or skill could manage.

Unfortunately, it didn't seem that there would be very many of those chances for either of them.

Another week went by. Blade began to wonder if Lord Desgo had thought up a new form of torture—leaving them alone until they either got ulcers from worrying about what might happen, or died of boredom because nothing did.

Neena laughed at the idea. "Things will happen, sooner or later. King Furzun is a mighty eater and drinker. He can eat and drink in a single day much more than even his body will hold. Then he must lie in bed for a week or more, bathed each day in perfume, drinking nothing but water, and taking not even one woman. Doubtless we came to Trawnom-Driba just after Furzun took to his bed. So nothing will be done about us until Furzun has seen us, and he will not see us until he is on his feet again."

The next morning breakfast was delivered at the usual time, in the usual buckets, and consisting of the usual stew. But five of the guards in blue leather stood behind the two slaves who lowered the buckets. All the guards'

46

leather gleamed with fresh wax, and the metal of their helmets and swords was freshly burnished.

Blade jerked a thumb at the guards. "All prettied up for a visit by somebody important, it seems. King Furzun?" Neena's mouth was full of stew, but she nodded.

They had just finished breakfast, when a terrific uproar of very badly blown trumpets sounded outside. Each of the trumpeters seemed to be playing in a different key. Several of them ran out of breath halfway through the fanfare. It was a dreadful noise. Neena winced and clapped her hands over her ears.

Eventually the uproar died away in a last pathetic flurry of gasps and feeble tootings. A bellowing voice roared out, "Furzun the Third, Supreme Warlord of All Trawn, Master of the Forests, Terror of Gleor—" The bombastic list of titles went on for quite a while. The herald's voice was no more musical than the trumpets, and it sounded as if he had a bad cold in addition.

In time, the herald ran out of titles for King Furzun or out of breath. Then the guards drew aside to the right and the left. Lord Desgo appeared in the doorway, and beside him one of the ugliest men Blade had ever seen.

King Furzun must have weighed close to four hundred pounds, most of it fat. He was nearly six feet tall—also six feet wide and six feet thick. He wore a dark yellow robe trimmed with brown fur and large enough to make a good-sized tent. The robe showed several patches and at least a dozen different kinds of food and wine stains. Furzun's long gray hair was stiff with grease and stood straight up. His long gray beard was even stiffer, and stood straight out from his chin like the bowsprit of a sailing ship. A sickeningly sweet odor of perfume rose from him in waves almost strong enough to beat down the smells of the prison chamber.

Beside him a naked slave girl knelt on the floor. She carried a basket in her mouth, like a dog carrying a bone. Occasionally Furzun would reach down into the basket, pick up a sweetmeat, and pop it into his froglike mouth.

Lord Desgo bowed to the king and pointed at Neena.

47

"Behold, Your Majesty. I spoke the truth when I said I had made Neena of Draad prisoner and gift to you. Indeed it is she who stands before us."

Furzun's eyes shifted in their deep pouches of fat and focused on Neena. "It is indeed Neena of Draad, and I spoke ill when I said you lied." Furzun's voice was the only normal, healthy thing about him. It was a plain, unaffected baritone, with a slight wheeziness about it.

"How came you to take her?" Furzun went on. "She is much given to hunting. This we know. But King Embor has his wits about him, and keeps a strong guard around her."

"It was not about her when we met," said Desgo. "Only her woman Kubona, whom I gave to my warriors for their pleasure." Blade saw Neena's mouth tighten into a hard line at that grim memory. "The man was a stranger to her, though he did fight for her. Yet he was no problem, for my stolof and I found it easy to overcome him."

"That part of your tale is most probably a lie," said Furzun. "He does not look like a man who would be easy for you to beat, with or without a stolof. However, we do have him a prisoner, and doubtless some use may be found for him. As for Neena, she was a fool to wander in the Forests of Gleor without a guard stronger than men's desires for her." Neena glared at the word "fool," and Blade laid a hand gently on her shoulder to calm her.

"Indeed, Your Majesty, she was a fool." Another glare from Neena. "Now she shall pay a woman's price for being foolish. She has been kept as she came to us, that you might treat her as one would write upon fresh-cleaned parchment. She has not even received any training."

Furzun nodded and pulled at the flesh of his jowls as he looked at Neena. Blade saw that she was beginning to breathe heavily in growing rage under Furzun's stare. Again he laid a hand on her shoulder. This time she twisted sharply, throwing his hand off.

"See how she moves," exclaimed Lord Desgo. "There is nothing she is not fit for. I can see that she would be

48

most marvelous in the Seven Blowing Reeds position, also the Flight of the Kingfisher, possibly the—" Lord Desgo went on and on, running through what sounded like Trawn's equivalent of the *Kama Sutra*. Furzun looked at Neena and listened silently as Desgo rambled on.

Blade kept looking from the men in the doorway to Neena and back again. Neena's nostrils were wide, and her neat firm breasts were rising and falling as her breathing quickened. That red-pepper temper of hers was slowly building up to an explosion.

Finally Lord Desgo noticed how excited Neena was. He broke off his listing of sexual gymnastics to point dramatically at Neena. Blade's ruby ring flashed on his hand as he shouted, "Look, Your Majesty. See how perfect she will be for your desires, how ready to meet them. My simple listing of what may be done to her has aroused her. She pants like a bitch in heat. She—"

Neena's temper exploded in an ear-splitting wordless screech that made Blade jump. Before he could move to stop her, she darted across the prison. Her hands locked around Lord Desgo's ankles. "You filthy pimp!" she shrieked. Before anyone could move she drove both her feet hard against the wall and heaved. She put every muscle in her body into that heave. Lord Desgo was jerked off his feet and over the edge of the doorway. He let out a yell of rage as he fell and a yell of pain as he landed. Then Neena was swarming all over him, kicking him, punching him, slapping his face, spitting on him. She was in a terrifying rage. Blade was sure that if Lord Desgo had been wearing a sword, Neena would have snatched it from his belt and cut his throat with it.

If the situation hadn't been so dangerous, Blade would have roared with laughter at Lord Desgo's humiliation. He knew that the sensible thing to do would be to step forward and pull Neena off Lord Desgo, before her rage provoked King Furzun into ordering both of the prisoners killed. What he *felt* like doing was stepping forward and helping Neena finish off the warrior noble. He felt his hands itching to close around Desgo's thick neck and squeeze and squeeze and squeeze—

A roaring sounded in Blade's ears. He looked up, to see King Furzun leaning against one side of the doorway, laughing until his stomach shook like jelly and tears streamed down his face and dripped from his beard. As his eyes met Blade's he lurched upright and shouted to someone standing outside. The guards on either side hastily backed out of Blade's sight.

A moment later a stolof-whistle sounded, and a moment after that came the chittering, clattering, and hissing of one of the monsters. Blade darted toward Neena, ready to pull her out of the way. If he could then grab Lord Desgo and use him as a shield—

Before Blade took three steps not one but two stolofs loomed up in the doorway. Both stood more than six feet high, and both were a deep, rich gold all over, instead of green. King Furzun stepped clear as the two stolofs shoved their heads forward and fired their sticky ribbons at Blade.

As before, they were excellent shots. One ribbon caught Blade by the left leg, the other caught him by the right arm. The stolofs reared back, and Blade was unceremoniously heaved forward onto his nose in the filthy mud. Cursing, he clawed and heaved at the ribbons as the two monsters reared back again. Blade was dragged forward toward the wall.

The stolofs heaved again, pulling Blade hard up against the wall, then once more. With the last heave, Blade rose completely clear of the ground and hung grotesquely against the wall. Neena leaped back from the sprawled Lord Desgo. Her face was twisted now with fear for Blade as well as hatred of the warrior noble.

The stolofs heaved one more time, and Blade rose until he hung just below the edge of the doorway. A vast hairy face peered over the edge at him. It was King Furzun.

"Look upon this man, princess," he snapped. "Look upon him well, where he is, and how he is at the mercy of the royal stolofs and the royal guards. For this attack of yours upon our servant Lord Desgo, he will hang head down for a day before the people of this city. The next time you lose your temper, the royal executioners will have a chance to practice upon him. Consider whether you wish this, or whether you wish to control your temper."

Neena said nothing, but her eyes were murderous. Blade found himself looking up at Furzun's grotesque face with more interest than before. Furzun had hit on by far the best way to keep Neena in line without threatening or hurting her directly. Lurking inside the mass of fat was a fairly shrewd mind.

The ribbons tightened again, jerking Blade up over the edge of the doorway, to sprawl on his back at King Furzun's feet. King Furzun smiled triumphantly. Then a club smashed down on Blade's head, and he didn't see or hear or feel anything for quite a while.

Chapter 9

King Furzun kept his promise. When Blade awoke, he was hanging head down, in a public place.

Four thick strands of stolof ribbon were tied to a heavy wooden beam that jutted out from a tower on the wall around the royal palace. Two strands were looped around each of Blade's ankles, so that he swung gently back and forth in the breeze like a hanging lantern. His head was throbbing painfully, but as far as he could tell he was otherwise unhurt. That wouldn't last long, of course. The people of Trawn were far too fond of tormenting helpless victims to pass up this opportunity.

Much less happened than Blade expected. People stopped to look at him, and hurled curses and clods of mud and manure up at him. But he hung too high—nearly fifty feet above the ground—to be easily hit, and no one ever seemed to stay around long enough to aim accurately.

Being fifty feet up also gave Blade a good view of the royal palace and the area around it. His throbbing head, dripping sweat, and stinging insects all blurred his vision, but what he saw he remembered.

The palace sprawled over about five acres in the southern end of Trawnom-Driba, only a few hundred yards from the city wall and ditch. On three sides lay a tangle of huts, sheds, and warehouses. On the fourth side was the broadest street Blade had seen in the city, lined with large buildings built of stone or gaudily painted wood.

At the foot of the wide street, just outside the palace wall, stood a massive square of smoke-blackened stone, forty feet on a side and ten feet high. It looked like nothing so much as a gigantic barbecue pit. The interior was half-filled with ashes and charcoal, sloping down to a dark hole in the exact center.

Blade paid no further attention to the stone square until afternoon. Then four guards led a dozen naked slaves up the steps on one side. The slaves carried large wooden scoops and wooden buckets. Half of them scrambled down into the pit and began shoveling the ashes and charcoal into the buckets. The other half began emptying the buckets into the hole in the center. Gray clouds of ashes swirled up, until the slaves were coughing so loudly that Blade could hear them from where he hung. The pit looked as if it were erupting like a small volcano.

Finally two slaves tied long heavy ropes around their waists. Three of their comrades took hold of each rope, the two slaves each picked up a scoop, and they were lowered down into the central hole and out of sight. They were down there for nearly an hour, and more clouds of ashes rose from the hole as they worked away.

During that hour Blade's mind went to work, arranging what he saw into a pattern. The pattern was extremely interesting.

The square of blackened stone was obviously for ceremonial fires. It was not far outside one wall of the palace. The unmistakable square bulk of the prison loomed not far inside that same stretch of wall.

Blade did a mental calculation of distance. If a straight line were drawn from the prison to the fire pit, it might cover about the same distance as the tunnel, from the grating to where the light came down from above. If the hole in the center of the pit was the hole at the far end of the tunnel, that could account for the orange glow he and Neena had seen. When the pit was heaped with blazing wood, light and heat would be pouring down the hole in the center, into the tunnel.

The tunnel might lead out to the hole in the center of the pit. The hole itself was large enough to let a man pass. That meant— No, there was still a maddening lot of unanswered questions. Unanswerable, too—at least for the moment. But that could change in time. Blade deliberately put any further thoughts of escape through the tunnel out of his mind, and let himself drift off into a half-doze. That was as close to sleep as he could manage while hanging head down like a bat in a cave.

The glow of sunset in his eyes and the clattering of wood on wood awoke Blade. The whole western horizon was a sheet of color, with a few clouds glimmering high above in the pale evening sky. A score of slaves were unloading logs from three carts and piling them up in the stone pit. Guards watched the slaves, and several noble warriors watched the guards. Blade recognized Lord Desgo among the nobles.

The logs were piled several layers thick. Then two more slaves poured a bucket of something thick and black into the pit. Lord Desgo climbed the steps, stood on the rim, then struck a light with flint and tinder. A quick flick of his arm, and the little flame arched down into the pit. Flames roared up thirty feet high. Lord Desgo scrambled down the steps and stood watching the flames as they settled down to a steady blaze.

Blade was sure of one thing, now. The tunnel from the prison did lead under the fire pit. The flames crackling and flaring up from the wood had the same orange color he and Neena had seen the week before. It was unmistakable.

Blade felt a shiver in the beam from which he was hanging. He twisted his head around to look toward the tower. Two of the blue-clad royal guards were turning a

53

crank, slowly swinging the beam in toward the tower. As Blade came within their reach, the two guards grabbed Blade by the arms. Two more reached up and grabbed him around the knees, while a fifth drew his sword and slashed through the stolof ribbons. With a mighty heave all five hauled Blade up over the railing. The rough wood scraped and bruised his skin, and he fell with a painful crash on the floor of the tower room.

The guards promptly hobbled his ankles and bound his hands behind his back. As they dragged him to his feet, footsteps sounded on the stairs of the tower. The guards turned Blade around, to face Lord Desgo.

Seen close up, the warrior noble was almost a comic sight. Neena had worked him over very thoroughly. He sported two beautiful black eyes and spectacular blue and purple bruising on almost every visible inch of skin.

Desgo looked Blade up and down, apparently hoping for some signs of pain or weakness. An unmistakable look of disappointment crossed his battered face when he couldn't find anything. His puffed lips twisted in a grimace.

"Well, slave," Desgo said. "Shall we have better behavior from you in the future, or shall you have more punishment from us?"

"It shall be as you wish," said Blade, keeping his head bowed.

"Good. That is the answer of a slave with some common sense about his lot." Desgo jerked a thumb over the railing toward the fire pit and its blazing logs. "You see that?"

"I do."

"I do, *Master*," said Desgo sharply. His hand dropped to a heavy club that he wore slung from his belt.

"I do, Master."

"That is the Hearth of Tiga, the Earth Mistress. It is a service to Tiga to provide slaves to cleanse her hearth and return the ashes to her. Do you understand?"

"Not altogether, Master."

"You are a stupid slave. But even stupid slaves can learn. I have suggested to King Furzun that you shall be

54

among the slaves that tend the Hearth of Tiga. I promise you that you shall work the hardest among all of them."

"I am grateful, Master." Blade certainly was! Desgo was sending him to the very place he needed to explore, the place that might offer him and Neena an escape route. But would they leave him and Neena together?

"Perhaps you are," said Desgo. "But I do not think your gratitude will last very long after you begin work." He turned sharply and stamped away down the stairs.

Four more royal guards clattered up the stairs, seized Blade, and half led, half dragged him away. They went down the stairs so fast that Blade, his legs still shaky from his day's hanging, stumbled several times. Each time he went down with bruising crashes, each time he was dragged to his feet by the laughing guards.

He began to feel better when he saw that he was being led back toward the prison. They led him on briskly, past three massive brick buildings with barred windows. From those windows the acrid smells and high-pitched chitterings of stolofs drifted out into the evening air.

They left the stolof pens behind them, passed four torch-lit buildings that seemed to be barracks, then turned into the street that led to the prison. The guards at the great door thrust it open as Blade approached. Then the same routine as before—two quick sword slashes to free Blade's hands and feet, and a quicker heave to send him flying forward into the darkness.

This time Blade was prepared for it. He landed rolling, stopped, and sat up. The door above slammed shut. He heard a faint stirring in the dimness.

"Neena?" Even if they'd thrown him back into the prison chamber, they might have already taken her out, to be prepared for King Furzun.

"Blade?" The voice, thank God, was unmistakable. As his eyes adjusted to the darkness, Blade saw Neena's slim form gracefully uncoil itself from a corner and come toward him.

She sat down beside him and ran her hands over his face and chest and arms, feeling him for wounds or perhaps just assuring herself that he was really back again. "Blade?" she said again.

"Yes." Blade was still feeling groggy, but the pain and dizziness and disorientation were all gone now. He felt only a healthy exhaustion, and he knew that the wisest thing to do would be to give in to it. What he *might* have discovered could wait until tomorrow.

"Lord Desgo decided I ought to serve—in the Hearth of Tiga. That's their—earth goddess. The hearth is where the fire—the fire was." His lips felt stiff and hard to move, as if they'd been bruised like Lord Desgo's.

Blade managed to lower himself backward onto the floor. He lay there, staring up at the slowly fading lights in the ceiling. As they faded out, he felt the warm, smooth firmness of Neena curling up against him, one arm across his chest and her hair flowing over his throat.

Chapter 10

When Blade awoke, he felt ready to tackle a day's work in the Hearth of Tiga or anywhere else Lord Desgo might decide to send him. He was no longer quite as immune to fatigue and strain as he had been when he left Oxford some years back. He was still in superb physical condition, though. There was practically nothing that a night's sleep couldn't remedy.

In her sleep Neena sensed that Blade was awake, opened her eyes, stretched like a cat, and reached up one hand to gently tug his bristling growth of beard. He gently took her hand in one of his and stroked her neck with the other. He felt refreshed and restored, but he also felt just as ready to lie here comfortably for the rest of the day, with Neena beside him.

"The fire showed in the tunnel again last night," she said. "It was burning even before they brought you back." Her voice was so low that Blade practically had to read her lips in order to understand what she was saying.

56

Blade only nodded, and drew one finger gently across her lips in a gesture he hoped she'd understand. That was absolutely final confirmation that the tunnel led under the Hearth of Tiga. It was also absolutely necessary for them to say nothing about the escape plans except when they were far down inside the tunnel, beyond anyone's hearing. By now the listeners above must suspect that the prisoners were entering the tunnel. But as long as those listeners continued to believe that the prisoners had no way of escaping through the tunnel, they wouldn't care greatly.

Before either Blade or Neena could say anything more, the door crashed open. Three guards heaved down a rope ladder and stood at its head with drawn swords.

"Tiga's waiting for your service," snapped one of them.

Neena's face hardened. Blade sprang to his feet and bowed. "Yes, Masters, I come." He scuttled across the floor to the ladder and scrambled up it.

All day long he did his best to keep up the same pose—a cringing, servile slave who had lost all of his courage and spirit through his punishment and his fear of more. It was not always easy. The work was exhausting, he was continuously being set to new tasks, he was given neither food nor water, and the guards were very free with the whip whenever they thought he was slowing down. There were times when it was hard not to pick up the nearest guard and throw him into the pit that yawned in the center of the Hearth of Tiga. Blade kept his mouth shut, his hands to himself, and his eyes continuously examining the hearth.

Just before sunset the guards gave Blade a bucket of water to drink. Then they threw two more buckets over him and led him back to prison.

Neena insisted on giving up her portion of dinner to Blade. It was not until well after the meal that they were able to slip away down the tunnel and speak openly.

"Neena, I thank you. But you must not do it again."

"Blade, you are going to be working very hard. You must have whatever you need to keep your strength up."

"Indeed, I must keep my strength up. So must you.

57

Our hope of escaping depends on how far you can jump and how well you can hold a rope. You will not remain strong enough for that if you starve yourself."

There was silence in the darkness of the tunnel, then faint, muffled sounds. Blade strained to make them out, then realized that Neena was fighting hard not to cry. He reached out and drew her against his chest. She lay warmly against it until she regained control of herself. Then she straightened up. Even in the darkness, Blade could sense that she was staring hard at him.

"Have we a way out of here, truly? Have you found where the tunnel goes? Can we get out through it?" Her questions came one after another. She wasn't quite as calm as she wanted to seem.

He gently took her chin in one hand. "Slow down, Neena. Don't let your hopes run ahead of what we know."

"But what *do* you know?"

He told her, leaving out nothing, including all the uncertainties that remained. "The ashes are dropped into a hole in the center of the hearth. The hole is covered with an iron grating, with bars set wide enough apart to let a man pass through easily.

"The hole leads to an underground pit. I don't know for certain how large or deep it is. But all the ashes and debris from the hearth are thrown into it. That is part of the ritual —'returning the ashes to the womb of the Earth Mistress,' they call it."

"And the tunnel leads into that pit?"

"It must, or we wouldn't be able to see the light of the fires in the hearth through it. The problem is, I don't know how far down in the pit the tunnel enters it.

"I will find out for sure when it comes my turn to be a pit slave. They are lowered through the grating into the pit, with scoops to spread the ashes evenly. It is the dirtiest and most painful job in tending the hearth, so I am sure I will get more than my share of chances to do it."

"And then?"

"If the tunnel is in the right place, I will see about hiding
58

a rope in its mouth. That shouldn't be too hard, with the darkness and all the clouds of ashes down there."

"I see," said Neena. "Then when I leap across the gap I simply run down to the mouth of the tunnel, bring the rope back, and——"

"Haul me across," finished Blade, with a grin. "Exactly. It will take a lot of muscle and a lot of luck, but I think it's our best way out."

"Well, Blade, I think we have already had much luck. We have found each other, and we can trust each other. Is that not more luck than we could have expected to come our way?"

Blade had to admit she was right. His arms went around her, and they sat there in the darkness for some time. There was more comfort than passion in their embrace. Finally they rose and returned to the prison chamber to sleep.

Blade found himself on pit duty the very next day. All that he'd heard about its being the hardest job in the service of Tiga was perfectly true. It was dark and airless in the pit. The ashes poured down and rose up around him in stifling clouds. They got in his mouth and his nose, his hair and his eyes. He coughed and gasped and choked, his eyes watered continuously, and even his ears seemed to be clogged by ashes and soot. The rope around his waist jerked and twisted constantly, and at times it seemed about to cut him in two. It took all his concentration and toughness to keep alert and keep going. He succeeded, and by the end of the day he'd found out what he needed to know.

"We can do it," he said to Neena that night. They were in the tunnel, and she was combing his hair and beard with her fingernails, trying to get out at least some of the ashes and grit. "The tunnel enters the pit only about ten feet below the iron grating."

Neena didn't ask him how he was going to solve the last problem—finding a rope and getting it into the right place. Blade himself wasn't quite sure. The ropes used to lower and raise the pit slaves would be more than long enough. How to get hold of one? Just as important, how to get hold of one fast? King Furzun wouldn't wait forever before having Neena taken out of the prison and moved into his harem.

Blade was given no pit work during the next two days. Instead he was given a taste of just about every other job involved in tending the Hearth of Tiga, from mortaring up cracks in the stone blocks to piling up logs for the next ritual fires. Each day was fourteen hours or more of grim, sweating, filthy work, making demands on even Blade's enormous strength.

As tired as he became, Blade's ceaseless watch for an opportunity to snatch and hide a rope went on. Nothing could make him abandon that watch. The whole thing would have been far easier if Blade could have simply waited several weeks, until the guards had him tagged as a docile, harmless lout, a slave they hardly needed to watch. Then he could have a fair hope of getting away, if not with murder, at least with the rope he needed.

He also kept an eye open for any clues to other possible escape routes. Unfortunately nothing came of that. He saw no prospect of any other way out of both the prison and the palace, except the tunnel. Simply getting out of the prison would leave him and Neena inside the palace walls, surrounded by more guards than they could possibly hope to fight.

Outside the palace, on the other hand, they would have all of Trawnom-Driba to give them room for running and fighting. They would have to get over the city's ramshackle wall, of course, but beyond that lay the endless forests of Gleor. In those forests Neena at least was far more at home than the warriors of Trawn, made slow and clumsy by too many years of relying on the stolofs in any tight spot. Lord Desgo was considered a mighty warrior among the men of Trawn, yet Blade knew he could fight two or three men as good as the nobleman and have them all dead or down in a few minutes.

It was the stolofs that were the heart of Trawn's power. Neena had said so many times. The more Blade saw, the more he believed her. The great spider-creatures, the regular green ones and the golden ones from the royal stables, were monstrous and deadly fighting machines.

They were not so fast that a swift-footed man could not outrun them. But anyone who stayed to fight was almost certainly doomed. The eyes were vulnerable, so were the uppermost joints of the legs, and so was a small spot under the belly. Otherwise every square inch of a stolof was covered with the scales and plates of armor that would turn the sharpest sword blade or spear point in Gleor.

"Warriors of Draad have slain stolofs in battle," Neena had said. "But only a few, and not all of those have lived through their victories. It is a rare man who can strike at one of the vital spots and move away before the stolof or the men with it attack. Stolofs alone would be formidable, but we could learn to meet them. The men of Trawn alone would give us a stout fight, for they greatly outnumber us, and few of our own warriors are your equal. Together, the stolofs and the warriors of Trawn may some day rule all of Gleor." Her face clouded and her eyes closed in pain as she said that.

So Blade knew that he would fight Draad's battles if he ever had a chance. He also knew that he would never have that chance unless he and Neena found a way out of the city. His fate and hers hung, if not quite by a thread, at least by a rope.

Chapter 11

Blade worked on everything except pit duty for eight maddening days. At times he wondered if his plans and hopes had been discovered. Perhaps Lord Desgo knew every detail of what Blade was planning, and these work assignments were one more way of tormenting him.

On the ninth day Blade went back into the pits. He went down there every other day from then on. The days were also becoming warmer, for the season was moving onward, toward a stifling tropical summer.

Blade now knew the best way of snatching and hiding the indispensable rope. He was only waiting for the best possible chance, knowing that he could count on only one. A single incident could probably be written off as an accident. A second incident would probably arouse suspicion, a third would be condemning himself to death.

The day of Blade's fifth turn in the pits dawned even hotter and more stifling than usual. As the slaves were led out to the Hearth of Tiga, the guards were already streaming with sweat and trying to stay in the shade as much as they could. In fact, they seemed more interested in finding shade than in keeping an eye on the slaves.

The long rope, more than fifty feet of it, was tied around Blade's waist. Three of his fellow slaves grabbed it as Blade walked to the grating and looked down into the pit. The glare of the sun above made the darkness below look even deeper than usual.

Blade lowered himself down through the grating and hung from one of the bars. The three slaves holding the rope tightened their grip, and the leader nodded. Blade let go of the bar and felt himself sliding down into the dusty darkness below.

The usual cloud of ashes and soot rose around him as he landed. A moment later the wooden scoop thumped down beside him. He picked it up and went to work. He wanted to work normally for a while, to get the people on the surface nicely off their guard.

Five minutes, ten minutes, twenty. By now Blade moved about in a continuous choking fog of ashes. He was working half-blindly, shoving ashes steadily down the slopes of the great piles, deeper into the darkness. He'd seen those slopes before. He'd also seen the body of a pit slave who died when one of those slopes gave way under him. The slave had died in the darkness, suffocated under tons of ashes.

Blade worked still harder for another five minutes. Now he looked like a mud-covered statue as his sweat mixed with the ashes and soot all over him. His eyes, his nose, his mouth, every inch of his skin prickled and burned and itched.

He threw a quick look upward. Nobody was visible through the grating. The rope from above drooped slackly down over the bars of the grating, as though the three slaves on the other end were half-asleep.

There would never come a better moment. Blade dropped his scoop, reached up, clamped both hands tightly on the rope, then heaved with all his strength. As he did he threw himself backward with all his weight, and simultaneously let out a long, agonizing yell of total dreadful fear.

As he went over backward into the ashes, he felt a jerk on the rope as it flew out of the hands of the slaves. Then he heard it hissing over the bars and plopping down all around him. At the same time the ashes rose up even more thickly than before, in a blinding dark gray fog. For a moment Blade was completely unable to see anything in any direction. He had to hold his breath to keep from choking to death on the ashes.

If he couldn't see anything, that meant anyone looking down from above couldn't see anything either. Working by touch alone, Blade wound the rope into a tight coil, then untied it from around his waist. As the cloud of ashes slowly settled, he let out another convincing yell. He also raised his head, searching for the mouth of the tunnel.

There it was, just visible enough to make a decent target. Blade drew back his arm, held his breath, and threw. He knew he would have only one sure chance to get the rope into the right place. If he missed, the rope would fall back down into the ashes. He would never find it quickly enough.

Blade's eye was good. So was his throwing arm. The rope sailed straight to its target, vanishing into the tunnel with a faint thud. Blade coughed as loudly as he could, thrashing his arms and legs around to make the ashes rise up around him again. Occasionally he stopped coughing to yell frantically for help. All in all, he gave a remarkably good imitation of a man struggling desperately not to fall down one of the great ash slopes to certain death.

Eventually Blade's flounderings and shoutings stirred the heat-drugged men above to help him. Another rope came snaking down through the grating, this one with a large loop tied in one end. Blade drew the loop over his head and shoulders and gave three tugs on the rope. The loop tightened around Blade's chest, and he rose out of the ashes and the pit into the daylight.

His head banged against one of the bars as he rose through the grating. Then the slaves and one of the guards were grabbing him by whatever came to hand, including his hair, and pulling him onto solid ground. He lay there, head swimming and chest heaving, until somebody dashed a bucket of water into his face.

Blade staggered to his feet, spluttering and gasping convincingly. Two of the slaves held him up until he was sure that he could stand by himself.

"Slope fall?" asked one of them.

Blade only nodded. Nobody would be expecting him to give a speech minutes after he had narrowly escaped being buried alive in ashes!

"All right, all right!" shouted one of the guards. "Stop playing around! You've had your bath. Now get back down there and get back to work!" A long whip cracked out, and the metal-weighted tip caught Blade across the hip. He gritted his teeth, felt the blood flowing, but also felt immensely relieved.

None of the guards seemed to have noticed anything wrong. To them it was just another near-accident to a slave. Why should that hold up the day's work any more than necessary?

The guards kept Blade an hour later than usual that day, to make up for the time he'd lost during the accident. After fifteen hours in the heat and the ashes and the darkness Blade was beginning to feel unsteady on his legs. The water they poured over him had never felt better, and the water they gave him to drink tasted like nectar from the gods. He was clearheaded and walking straight by the time the guards led him back to his prison.

The guards threw him down into the chamber as usual, and Neena ran to help him to his feet, also as usual.

"You look—" She shook her head, unable to find words. "What happened?"

"A slope collapsed under me in the pit," Blade said

aloud. Ignoring the raucous laughter of the guards, he took her in his arms and held her, his mouth half-muffled in her hair, close to one ear. They stood that way until the guards' laughter died away and the door slammed shut.

"You did it?" she whispered.

"I did. The rope is in place."

She shivered. "Is something wrong?" he asked.

"The day after tomorrow—they come for me—they take me to King Furzun. The guards said it."

"Then we escape tonight."

"No, Blade—you must have a day to become strong again."

Blade shook his head. "That won't help, and tomorrow night will be more dangerous. They'll be expecting you to do something desperate. Tonight they'll be thinking you're paralyzed with fear."

"But "

"It will be tonight, Neena. If it is not tonight, it may not be at all."

Neena shivered, then forced a faint, wavering smile onto her face.

"Very well, Blade, it shall be tonight."

Chapter 12

Darkness came to the world outside their prison. Blade and Neena ate dinner, then rested, gathering as much strength as they could for their escape.

Blade had a grimly accurate notion of their chances. This whole escape was a thoroughly improvised affair, full of gambles, with little equipment and less margin for error. They would have no weapons, no clothing, no footwear. They would have practically nothing except a grim determination not to die helplessly in Trawn. How far that determination could carry them remained to be seen.

Beside him, Neena was drifting off to sleep. It was a

good sign that she was calm enough to sleep. Blade remained awake and watched the tunnel. He did not expect to see the orange glow of a fire in the Hearth of Tiga. No wood had come in for one during the day. That was also good. The fire that had helped them before by showing them the gap could now trap them in the tunnel.

Neena slept peacefully, and her low, regular breathing even lulled Blade into a few minutes' doze. He jerked himself awake, shook his head to clear it, then gently awakened Neena.

"It is time."

She sat up, brushed the hair out of her eyes, shook herself, stretched like a cat, loosening every muscle, and nodded.

As silently as prowling animals they crept across the floor toward the grating and opened it. Blade took two of the wooden bars with him. Win or lose, they would not be back here.

They moved down the tunnel, Neena leading. Blade found himself fighting not to hold his breath. He accidentally put a hand down on Neena's ankle, and heard her give a small "yip" of surprise and fright. She was obviously just as nervous as he was.

The tunnel seemed to go on forever. At last Blade felt Neena stopping in front of him and reaching out with one hand to probe the darkness ahead.

"We're there."

Blade crawled forward, until he sensed that he was on the edge of the gap. Slowly he stood up, arms probing on either side, then above him. He was standing where he'd intended to, far enough from the edge to have firm ground underfoot, yet close enough to have a high ceiling overhead. A good starting point, but that was all. Neena would literally have to make a leap in the dark, with a three-hundred foot drop to certain death below her if she missed.

Blade turned to Neena, sensing her rather than seeing her standing in the darkness beside him. She was breathing deeply.

"Are you ready?"

66

"Yes."

She stepped in front of him and he knelt down and caught her about the waist. Blade told himself that they'd rehearsed the positions half a dozen times, that everything should go right.

You haven't rehearsed going through with it, a voice in his head reminded him. He told the voice to shut up. In his arms he felt Neena tensing, crouching down for her leap. Blade dug in his heels to get a firmer footing, then squeezed Neena's thigh.

"Now?"

"Now."

All of Blade's muscles and all of Neena's uncoiled in a split second surge of controlled power, as the man and the woman shot up from their crouch. Blade felt Neena leave his arms, felt his toes come down on the very edge of the gap, felt earth start to crumble beneath him, and threw himself backward. He landed with a thud and his head smashed into the packed earth of the tunnel floor hard enough to half stun him. His head still spinning, he sat up and looked out across the invisible gap to the equally invisible far side.

He hadn't heard the sound of a safe landing, but he hadn't heard the dreadful death-scream of someone plunging down three hundred feet either. Then from the darkness he heard a faint "Ouch!"

"Neena? Are you all right?" Blade had intended to whisper. His voice came out in a roaring bellow that went echoing away up and down the tunnel.

The words he'd been hoping to hear came out of the darkness. "Yes, I've landed all right. Just a moment—" Another "Ouch!" "I think I've sprained a finger and a couple of toes. That's all. I'm going to crawl down and get the rope now."

"Good."

There was the sound of bare feet and hands scrabbling away down the tunnel, fading away into a new silence. Blade waited. If the rope wasn't where Neena could get to it, the escape was doomed and Neena herself would be trapped in the tunnel, unable to return across the gap or climb upward to freedom.

A foot scraped on hard earth in the darkness. Blade stiffened.

"Neena?"

"Yes. I've got the rope. You can throw the stake across now."

Blade picked up the two wooden bars and heaved. Two soft thumps were followed by another "Ouch!"

"One hit me on the shin," said Neena. Blade laughed, the first time he'd been able to do that since entering the dark tunnel tonight.

Thudding and thumping noises followed, as Neena tried to drive the stake into the floor of the tunnel. The noises went on for quite a while. Finally—

"It's not in very deep. The floor's too hard."

"Think it will hold?"

"It had better."

There was nothing more to say. A faint hiss in the darkness, and something fell beside Blade with a soft thump. He bent down and touched the rope.

Carefully he tied a small loop in his end of the rope, to give himself a better grip. Then:

"All right, Neena—pull in the rope until I call." The rope in Blade's hands started to tighten. "All right. I'm coming over now."

Blade sat down on the edge of the gap, his legs dangling down into empty space. There was just enough slack left in the rope to provide a loop around his chest. He checked everything once more, took a firm grip on the rope, and slid off into space.

He swung down into the gap, seeming to float through the silence and darkness all around him. He thrust his legs out in front of him to take the shock of striking the far wall. He had a moment's impression that he'd stepped off into a whole new realm of space and would go swinging on through it for the rest of time.

His feet slammed hard into the far wall. He heard clods of earth break free and fall. He shifted his grip on the rope slightly, ready to start climbing up hand over hand.

68

Then the rope shivered, and a sharp cry came from above. "The stake's pulled loose. The rope's—" Blade didn't need any more words from Neena to know what was happening to the rope. Inch by inch it was sliding downward, carrying him with it. Eventually the end would pass through Neena's hands, and after that—

Blade was already acting as he thought, gouging at the wall with both feet, working furiously to dig out a foothold. He managed to make one that would take at least one foot. He jammed his left foot in hard, and the deadly sliding of the rope stopped for a moment.

The rope tightened in his hands, then there was a thump from above and it drew even tighter. Neena's breathing turned into painful gasps.

Cautiously Blade shifted his foot. The rope went still tighter. Neena gasped again, but Blade did not sink down. He began to work his way up the rope, moving one hand at a time. Each movement drew another gasp from Neena. But the rope held.

The minutes that it took Blade to make the twenty-foot climb seemed like hours. Eventually he reached up and his hand came down on hard level ground. He felt for one handhold, then for another, shifting all his weight onto his arms. There was a sigh of blissful relief from Neena. Blade hung for a moment, then heaved himself upward with all the strength in both massive arms. He flew up over the edge like a cork coming out of a champagne bottle and sprawled flat on his stomach—squarely on top of Neena. She gasped again. He hastily rolled off her and reached out to her.

She lay on her side on the floor, face toward the gap, several coils of the rope drawn snugly about her waist and hips. She'd thrown herself down and used her own body to anchor the upper end of the rope. The rope had squeezed and pinched and bruised her every time Blade moved. Even worse, it had dragged her slowly and steadily toward the edge. When Blade reached the top, there had been barely a foot to go before she reached the edge and they both fell down into the darkness together.

Blade sat beside Neena for some time, catching his

breath and letting the princess catch hers. He wondered how to thank her adequately for her display of courage and quick thinking. In the end he said nothing, simply took her hand and squeezed it. Then he coiled up the rope and they moved on.

Side by side they crawled down to the mouth of the tunnel in the great pit under the Hearth of Tiga. The night was overcast, and no light came down through the grating overhead. A strong wind was blowing, and Blade could hear its whistles and moans clearly. The darkness and the wind would help hide the next stage of their escape.

Quietly he tied one end of the rope around one of the bars from the grating. Then he swung the rope around several times and heaved. The rope flew upward and dropped neatly over one of the bars of the grating. Blade and Neena froze, waiting to see if the sound would alert a guard. Nothing happened. Blade pulled hard on the rope, until the wooden bar was firmly wedged against the grating. The moment he felt that, he swung out over the pit and began swarming up the rope hand over hand, as fast as he could move.

He reached the grating, poked his head up through it, and looked around. The darkness and the wind made it hard to see or hear if anyone was lying in wait. He pulled himself the rest of the way up through the grating. Then he lay flat on the rough iron bars while he swung the looped end of the rope back toward Neena. She caught it on the second swing. Slowly Blade drew her up out of the pit, and in a few more seconds she lay beside him on the grating. In spite of her exhaustion and bruises, she was grinning widely and shaking with silent laughter.

It was too soon to celebrate, for there was still the city around them. But the luck they needed so badly had stayed with them so far. If it stayed with them for a few more hours—

Blade lifted his head to look around him again, then froze. Above them, on the wall of the Hearth of Tiga, was the unmistakable silhouette of an armed man.

Chapter 13

The guard would have to be taken out, swiftly and silently. Any noise or delay, and Blade and Neena would have half the palace guards swarming out after them.

Blade uncoiled the rope and adjusted the loop he'd made for climbing. Now it was large enough to fall over a man's head. He handed one of the wooden bars to Neena and pointed.

"I'm going to try getting him down here with this," he said, raising the rope. "You be ready to knock him over the head with the bar and take his clothing and gear."

Blade crept silently across the hearth until he could get a clear throw at the guard. The ashes underfoot and the wind blowing past above muffled his slow footsteps.

Once in position, Blade waited until the guard came to a stop and turned his back on the hearth. Then Blade sprang forward, whirling the rope around his head. It snaked through the air, twisting as the wind caught it, but still sailing straight to its target. The noose fell over the guard's head. Before he could move or cry out, Blade heaved. The noose tightened around the man's neck. He flew backward off the wall and fell with a muffled crash almost at Blade's feet.

The guard was still in midair as Neena sprang forward. She was beside him as he landed, smashing in his throat with the wooden bar. The man gave a choking gurgle, twisted and writhed for a moment, then lay still. Neena quickly began to strip off the guard's leather armor, weapons, and belt pouch.

Again they had a brief, nerve-wracking wait, to see if the alarm was up. In the windy darkness the guard's sudden disappearance seemed to have gone unnoticed.

The guard's armor was far too small for Blade's massive frame. So Neena put on the armor and belted on the sword. Then they tied the rope around Blade's neck, with

71

an easily slipped knot, and Neena took the other end in her free hand. To the casual observer it would look as if Neena was a guard leading a slave somewhere. This was the best disguise they could manage now. It might even be good enough to get them out of Trawnom-Driba, a city where the drastic penalties for being too curious made people very willing to mind their own business.

The wind increased steadily as they climbed down from the Hearth of Tiga and moved across the square in front of the palace. Instead of following the main street, they plunged into the tangle of huts, sheds, warehouses, and simple ruins that lay to the south of the palace. Blade relied on his sense of direction to get them safely through the twisting alleys of that quarter. There would be no one awake and about in those alleys, curious or otherwise.

The darkness among the buildings was almost as complete as it had been down in the tunnel. Blade moved up into the lead and Neena fell in behind him, eyes roving about and sword drawn. About halfway through the quarter they stopped to rest. They sat down in the shadow cast by an enormous pile of barrels. The barrels oozed black drops of something that looked and smelled like liquid tar. Blade recognized the liquid poured on the logs in the hearth, to produce the orange color in the flames of the ritual fires.

Blade leaned back against the barrels and took several deep breaths. Not much farther, and they would be at the last barrier before the safety of the forests. The guards on the outer wall would be more alert than any others in the city, although that wasn't—

The ragged blaring of trumpets and the thunder of drums reached them on the wind. The uproar swelled until it drowned out the wind, faded for a moment, then rose again. In the moment's lull, they could both hear angry shouting from the direction of the palace.

"Oh, blast," said Blade quietly. "The alarm's up." He sprang to his feet and looked at the stack of barrels. "Neena. Give me the firelighter from the guard's pouch, and keep clear."

"What—?" Neena began, then fell silent. She knew

Blade well enough by now not to waste time asking questions. Her sword rose, and she sprang back, eyes searching the darkness.

Blade threw the rope off his neck, bent down, and gripped one of the barrels. It must have weighed close to two hundred pounds. Slowly he lifted it and backed away from the pile. Then he raised the barrel high over his head and brought it smashing down on two other barrels. All three cracked open, and the dark tarry liquid flooded out.

Blade sprang clear, picked up a long splinter, dipped it in the liquid, then struck a spark with the firelighter. As the spark landed on the soaked splinter, it flared up with the familiar orange flame. Blade let the splinter burn for a moment, then flicked it away from him, squarely into the spreading pool of liquid.

The whole pool erupted in a sheet of orange flame and a crackling roar that drowned out both the wind and the alarm signals. For a moment Blade felt as though he was standing beside an open blast furnace. Then he turned and motioned for Neena to follow him. They plunged away into the no longer dark alleys. As they left the pile behind, Blade heard the barrels starting to explode, and saw the pillar of fire behind them climb still higher.

As they ran, doors and shutters began opening on either side of them and heads popped out to see what was going on. All eyes at once turned toward the fire. No one seemed to notice the small soldier and the oversized slave pounding past at a dead run.

"Why *did* you do that?" gasped Neena, as they turned down an alley that was still dark. "Now everyone will know which way we've gone."

"Maybe. But if we move fast enough it won't do them a bloody bit of good! This quarter's a tinderbox and it's right next door to the palace. There's a good blaze going, and the wind's blowing hard enough to spread the fire. I'm sure King Furzun would still like to have you for his harem. But I'm betting he'll risk letting you go rather than have his palace burn down around his ears."

73

Neena grinned wickedly. "I see. So all the guards will be running to put out the fire and not to catch us."

"We can damned well hope so," said Blade.

They slowed down as they gradually left the fire behind them. Twice they had to stop entirely so that Blade could get his bearings. The fire was already visibly spreading, and the wind was pushing it straight in the direction of the palace. They could hear a continuous roar and boom of flames.

They could also hear the mounting uproar caused by their escape. Trumpets and drums sounded all around them, louder than ever. Beyond the fire Blade could see the walls of the palace, and torches and blue lanterns darting back and forth along them. He hoped the guards would drop a few of those lanterns and torches and start another dozen fires!

The second time they stopped, Blade and Neena heard stolof-whistles joining the uproar. Neena's face turned pale under the dirt, but Blade only laughed.

"Why are stolofs so amusing now?" Neena snapped. She was obviously irritated with him as well as nervous about the monstrous hunter-creatures with their deadly ribbons.

Blade laughed again. "If I were running the hunt for us, I wouldn't let a stolof out of the pens tonight. There's enough confusion in the city already. Those stolofs aren't very bright, and they'll just add to the confusion if their masters aren't careful."

Eventually they found a path that turned sharply left, then ran into an alley. When they reached the alley, they stopped. Fifty feet farther on, the alley gave onto the open space between the quarter's buildings and the city wall. The towers of a gate rose above the roofs of the next row of the hovels and sheds. At the end of the alley stood three soldiers, all holding spears, all with their backs turned to the alley. Whatever they were watching for, they didn't expect it to come out of the alley.

Blade and Neena looked at each other. Blade hefted one of the wooden bars in each hand. Neena tied her helmet on the back of her head so that it wouldn't fall over her eyes and drew her sword. Then they plunged forward down the alley, as fast as their feet could cover the muddy ground.

The three soldiers had time to hear the footsteps and turn around. One had time to raise a spear, another had time to shout. Then Blade and Neena were on them.

Neena's sword leaped upward, straight into the throat of the soldier with the raised spear. He dropped the spear and clamped his hands on the sword. Neena twisted it in the wound, then jerked it free. The soldier gurgled, tried to clasp his hands over the gaping wound in his throat, then collapsed.

Blade swung one bar sideways to deflect a spear thrust, then smashed the other bar down on the arm of his other opponent. The man screamed and shifted his spear to his good hand. Blade struck the spear down, cracked the man hard across the jaw, then turned to guard his left side.

The man there made the mistake of raising his spear for a thrust downward. Blade dropped to a crouch, went in under the spear, and butted the man hard in the stomach. The breath went out of him with a *whoooof* and he slammed back against the wall behind him. Before he could thrust again, Blade swung a bar with all his strength. It smashed into the man's temple, knocking him sideways and down. Blade crashed a foot down on the man's ribs, then turned back to the soldier with the broken arm and jaw.

The man had more than that now. He lay flat on his back in the mud, and Neena was just pulling her sword out from between his ribs. Blade bent down and stripped off the man's belt with its sword and knife. Then he and Neena each picked up a spear. They dashed out into the open, crouching low and heading for the wall.

Seconds after they emerged, a flight of arrows whistled overhead and thudded into the dirt and the buildings behind them. None came near them. On a night this dark, the excited archers weren't going to be shooting very well. Like the stolofs, they were more likely to interfere with the hunt for the prisoners than help it.

And where were the stolofs, anyway? After all that whistling—

Blade had barely finished asking himself that question when Neena gave a shrill cry and grabbed his arm, pointing off to the right with her free hand. There came the stolofs, a pair of the great golden ones from the royal pens. Half a dozen soldiers ran beside and behind them, and ahead of them ran Lord Desgo himself, blowing his whistle and waving a sword in each hand.

The soldiers of Desgo's party saw the prisoners at the same moment. All of them dashed forward with wordless howls of rage and triumph. Desgo saw them do this, stopped dead, and was nearly knocked off his feet by the stolofs. He jumped to one side, spat out the whistle, and began shrieking orders to his men. All of them were too busy fighting to have obeyed even if they'd been able to hear him.

The six soldiers charged straight at Blade and Neena. Blade and Neena raised their spears and threw. Two soldiers went down, one pierced in the throat, the other with his thigh torn open. Blade and Neena didn't have time to retrieve their spears before the other soldiers were on them. So they stood back to back and went to work with their swords.

One of Blade's opponents ran after only a few blows. Blade was cutting and thrusting at the other man when Neena screamed behind him. He whirled, to see that Neena's two opponents had disarmed her and were grabbing her to drag before Lord Desgo.

Blade let out a roar of fury and launched a quick attack on his immediate opponent, a slash that opened the man's sword arm from wrist to elbow. Then he turned to save Neena. As he did, her two captors turned to face him, pulling her across in front of them to act as a shield against Blade's attack.

A moment later one of the stolofs launched its ribbons. As always, it was an excellent shot, but the ribbon fell neatly on one of the soldiers holding Neena, instead of on Blade or the princess. The stolof reared, and the soldier was jerked backward off his feet and dragged toward it.

76

Neena twisted out of the grip of the other soldier and drove her knee up into his groin. He doubled up with a howl just in time for the edge of Blade's hand to smash down on the back of his neck. Neena snatched up her sword again. She was so filled with the lust for combat that before Blade could stop her she dashed off after the soldier who'd been knocked down by the stolof. Blade was left alone for a moment, to meet Lord Desgo and the other stolof.

Blade closed with the nobleman until the stolof could not fire without entangling both of them in the ribbon. He feinted low, then went in over Desgo's guard and slashed at the man's head. Desgo twisted enough to keep his skull from being split apart, but Blade's sword slashed down from forehead to right jaw, just missing one eye. Desgo screamed, dropped his swords and whistle, and staggered, half-blinded by pouring blood. Blade grappled with him, drove one fist into his jaw and another into his stomach, then threw him to the ground.

Blade's ruby ring glinted like a drop of fire on Desgo's limp hand. Blade bent down, stripped the ring off, and put it back on the ring finger of his own left hand. That bastard Desgo wasn't going to get *anything* from him, except a quick death. Blade raised his sword, ready to drive it down into Desgo's chest.

Then Neena screamed, "Blade, the stolof!" Before Blade could move, a ribbon fell across his back and left shoulder. Blade whirled and saw at once that Desgo's stolof had made a fatal mistake. It had come too close.

Before the creature could rear back and pull Blade off his feet, Blade closed in. He dashed straight between the forelegs and thrust over the dripping mandibles, squarely into the center of the three glaring red eyes.

The stolof jerked convulsively and let out a hissing scream. Foul-smelling yellowish fluid gushed out of the wound, stinging where it fell on Blade's skin. He stepped back.

Neena stood in front of the other stolof now, waving a dripping sword at it, shrieking curses. The stolof seemed paralyzed, its master silent and its comrade (or mate?)

77

dying. There were no other soldiers in sight on the ground, and only a few on the wall. Blade had no doubt where all the others had gone. The fire he'd set was now roaring up in a solid wall of flame a quarter of a mile long, sweeping steadily toward King Furzun's palace.

The few soldiers still in sight were manning the gate, though, and there were archers among them. Blade scanned the area for some other way over the walls, and his eyes fell on the stolof facing Neena. It stood almost next to the wall, and rose halfway up it.

Blade snatched up a fallen spear and dashed toward the creature. He came in from the side, drove the spear point into the ground, and pole-vaulted up onto the stolof's back. For a moment he had to fight not to slide right off again. Then he braced himself and shouted.

"Neena! Here!"

The princess heard him, turned, and sprang toward the stolof. Blade bent down as she leaped, heaving her up beside him on the creature's back. Before its sluggish wits could react to what was happening, Blade practically threw Neena up onto the walkway of the city wall. As the stolof started to move, Blade caught the railing and heaved himself up after Neena.

He'd held onto his spear, and it was a good thing that he had. Someone in the gate tower shouted, and someone else let fly with an arrow. It came uncomfortably close. Before the archer could shoot again, Blade picked him out from among his comrades and hurled the spear. It was a long shot, but Blade's eye and arm had a machine's precision tonight. The archer staggered as the spear drove into his thigh just below his armor, then toppled back against the tower railing. It gave with a crack and he vanished from sight with a scream, to land with a splash in the water-filled ditch below.

Blade turned and sprang up onto the outer railing of the wall. Neena joined him. The darkness beyond the ditch looked friendly and welcoming. Neena squeezed Blade's hand briefly, then they both leaped out and down, aiming for the far side of the ditch.

It was a long jump and a long drop, but they both

78

landed safely. Blade felt as though every bone in his body and all the teeth in his mouth had been jarred loose from one another. But he sprang instantly to his feet and helped Neena up. In a few more seconds they were on the move, heading away from the city into that friendly darkness at a dead run.

They ran and they ran and they ran. Gradually the roar of the flames, the trumpets and drums of the soldiers, the shouts of angry or frightened people faded behind them. Gradually the forest grew thicker around them and behind them. Even the glow of the great fire faded away. They ran on, with no sound but their footsteps, their breathing, and the *chirrr* of night insects.

They ran on, until finally neither of them could have gone a step farther if all the stolofs in Trawn had been at their heels. Blade barely had the strength to find a concealing clump of bushes and carry Neena to it. Then he lay down beside her and let sleep take him.

It was a more pleasant sleep than he'd known since he'd entered this dimension. For the first time he was free.

Chapter 14

The jungle awoke the next morning in a hideous uproar of bird cries, animal howls, the squalling and squealing of apes, the *clak* and drone of insects. The uproar jerked Blade up out of sleep like an alarm signal. Neena awoke more slowly, sat up and listened without even opening her eyes, then lay back down and drifted off to sleep again. Either her trained ears hadn't caught anything in all the uproar that might mean danger, or she was too exhausted to care.

Blade let her sleep and listened more carefully himself. After a while he could pick out fifty or sixty distinct sounds from the jungle around him. None of them sounded at all human, or like the chittering of a stolof on the hunt.

Blade decided that Neena had the best idea, and lay down again. Here they had a good hiding place, and their night's run must have given them a good many miles' head start on any possible pursuit. If they spent the day here, they could be out again after dark, rested, refreshed, and far better prepared to face anything they might meet. Blade stretched out, closed his ears to the jungle sounds, and drifted off to sleep.

He awoke with the sun well down in the sky and the light creeping through the bushes already turning red. Neena was wide awake, combing leaves and debris out of her hair.

They ate sour greenish white berries from a trailing vine and drank at a small stream nearby. Neena took bearings on the setting sun. Then they went back under the bush and waited until darkness settled down over the forest.

"The stolofs can see and sense equally well by day or by night," she said. "The same is not true of their masters. Those of Trawn fear the forests by night. In a way, they are wise to do so. At night the forests of Gleor can be deadly to one who knows them not. I, on the other hand—"

"—have been at home in them since you were three years old?" Blade finished the sentence for her.

Neena laughed. "No, I was not allowed into the forest until I was nine. I have still spent ten years learning its ways. That is ten years more than most of the warriors of Trawn. Against ill luck there is no defense. Otherwise I think we shall come safely to my last camp, and then to the lands of Draad."

"Why your camp? Why not go straight home?"

"Blade, perhaps you wish to show how strong you are by roaming the forests of Gleor naked and practically unarmed. I have no such desire. In that camp I left spears, bows, clothing and boots, bottles for water, even some dried meat. There is also Kubona." Her face turned hard. "I cannot give her vengeance now, although she shall have it sooner or later. I can give her bones proper burial, and her spirit the prayers to speed its passing."

They left their hiding place as soon as it was fully dark. Neena led the way for a few hundred yards through a nightmarish tangle of vines and underbrush, to thoroughly confuse their trail. Then she swung west, onto a well-beaten animal trail, and once on the trail settled down to a steady trot.

They kept going all night, with only one short stop for rest and water and one short detour around a small hunters' camp. Shortly before dawn they drank again from a muddy pool and ate the meat of several fallen koba nuts. Then they scrambled forty feet up a spreading tree, found a perch screened by its long trailing leaves, and went to sleep.

For three more days and three more nights this pattern repeated itself. Once they found a pool large enough for them to bathe. Blade pulled a foot-long fish out of that pool, but Neena took one look at it and threw it back.

"A ti-ter fish," said Neena briefly. "Our hunters use the fluid from its liver and bladder to poison their arrows."

Another time they had to spend an hour of darkness perched high in a tree. At the foot of the tree a seventy-foot snake was curling up to sleep off a meal. When the snake hadn't moved for an hour, Blade and Neena crept down the tree and slipped silently away into the darkness.

Blade got a good look at the snake as they slipped past it. Its mouth was six feet wide, large enough to swallow a stolof or two or three men at one gulp.

On the fourth morning they did not seek out a hiding place for the day. Instead Neena took another set of bearings on the sun, then led the way off to the north.

"I think we shall be reaching the camp today," she said. "It will be easier to find it by day than by night, even for me."

"What about our friends from Trawn?"

"There is not much danger from them any more, I think. We are beyond where the hunters usually go. Anyone who has been chasing us from the city itself is certainly at least a day's march behind us."

Neena followed as straight a course as the jungle would let her until just before noon. Then she stopped and began casting back and forth like a hunting dog, looking for the marks she'd left to show the way back to the camp. As she did that, Blade kept his eyes roaming back and forth, scanning the jungle around them. Neena's contempt for the soldiers and hunters of Trawn made her willing to assume that they were all many miles away. Blade, stubbornly cautious, refused to share that assumption.

The day moved on toward noon. Neena led the way deeper and deeper into a particularly grim and gloomy stand of trees. Here there was nothing but centuries-old forest giants, their high canopies so thick that the forest floor underneath was perpetually dark and almost lifeless. The heat had a deadly, airless quality to it. Blade began to feel as though he was back in the ash pit under the Hearth of Tiga, slaving away in the stifling darkness.

Blade soon lost track of time. He was beginning to lose track of distance when suddenly Neena gave a sharp, wordless cry, almost a squeal. For a moment Blade wondered if she'd been bitten by a snake. She stiffened, then seemed about to dash wildly forward. He caught her arm. She let out her breath in a long sigh, then raised her other arm and pointed. Blade followed her gesture with his eyes and saw a huge hollow tree, gray and moss grown, split open on one side.

They had reached Neena's camp. Another part of their escape lay behind them. Only one more part lay ahead of them, and that should be the easiest one of all.

Blade and Neena stood side by side for another moment. Then they both broke into a run toward the hollow tree.

The weapons and gear lay well inside the dark hollow, further concealed under piles of leaves and vines.

"Kubona and I didn't want anyone from Trawn stumbling on them, of course," she said. "We also didn't want any of our own hunters from Draad finding them. I wasn't supposed to be this far out into the forest on my own."

Blade said nothing, and tried to keep his face straight. Apparently he wasn't entirely successful. Neena looked at him, then sighed.

"All right," she said. "There's no need to look at me that way. I know what you're thinking, and what you'd like to say. You're right, I'll admit it, so you can keep quiet. I'll have enough to listen to from my father when we get home."

"No doubt," said Blade, in a carefully neutral voice.

Neena shrugged. "I suppose I deserve at least some of it. Certainly it was my fault that Kubona was killed. But I suspect my father will be so happy that I'm home safe that he won't say *too* much. Queen Sanaya, on the other hand—"

"Your mother?"

"My—no, let's just call her my father's chosen wife." The chill in Neena's voice was unmistakable.

"Not much love lost between you and Sanaya, I gather?"

"Not enough for her to really regret my being carried off and enslaved in Trawn. She—" Neena hesitated, as if uncertain how much she should say, then went on quickly. "She is only three years older than I. My father married her two years ago, in the hope of getting from her more children, sons above all."

"You are King Embor's only heir?"

"There is my sister Jana. But she is only eleven, and my father does not care much for her. My mother died bearing her."

"Is there a law against women ruling in Draad?"

"There is no law, but it has not happened for two centuries. There are many of the warriors and clan chiefs who would be happier under the rule of a man. They say that a man will be a better leader in war against Trawn."

Blade frowned. "They are not thinking very clearly."

Neena spat on the forest floor and slammed her fist against the bark of the tree. "They are damned fools! Trawn will move against us much sooner than they think. If Sanaya were to conceive tonight, we would have war before her son was able to walk. Even if he has time to grow to the age of a warrior, he will only die with the rest of us if he can do nothing about the stolofs."

She sighed. "Ah, well, Sanaya will bear that son

sooner or later. She comes from a line where the women are always fertile. Then perhaps she will have less time to intrigue with her friends or worry about me."

There was everything Neena had promised in the camp, although the dried meat had developed worms. Blade was almost hungry enough to cut off the worm-infested portions and eat the rest, but not quite. Not when they would have fresh roast meat in a few more hours.

Neena's first concern, however, was final rites for Kubona, putting her body or at least her spirit to rest. "Those swine of Desgo's just left her lying like a piece of meat when they'd finished with her," Neena said. There was a note of killing rage in her voice, so that even Blade felt uncomfortable for a moment. "The gods alone know what may have been by there since our fight. Well, we shall do our best."

The place of the fight and Kubona's death lay another two miles away, on the far side of the thick stand of trees. Neena led the way swiftly through the shadows, and they reached the river bank by midafternoon.

The skeletons of two of the soldiers from Desgo's band still lay bleaching in grass now grown a foot high around them. Neena and Blade searched carefully, hoping to turn up Kubona's more delicate bones somewhere. They found nothing that could have been her. Even her clothing and weapons had vanished.

"Perhaps a party from Draad found her and took her back for burial," said Blade.

Neena shrugged. "Perhaps. The odds are long against it. The hunters of Draad come forth more often and travel farther than those of Trawn. But the forests of Gleor are large, so it is still hard for them to find what they are not seeking.

"No, I think the beasts have given Kubona a forest burial. That is all she can hope to have, and we cannot hope to change what the gods have sent her." Neena sat on the grass, cross-legged, her chin in her hands and her eyes cast down on the ground.

After a moment she smiled and stood up. "Perhaps it has been for the best after all. Kubona was a huntress and the daughter of many hunters. Her soul belonged to the open air and the great forests. Now her body does also. Perhaps the gods knew what they were doing." She turned toward the patch of grass where Kubona had died. "Here we are, my comrade. Here we are, alive, to wish you peace now and avenge you when the chance comes."

Neena was speaking so intensely that Blade had the uncomfortable feeling she was speaking to a real presence—or at least to a presence that was real to her. He did not believe in ghosts, or that anything in this sunlit clearing could do him and Neena any harm. Rather, he felt that he was an unwanted intruder on a farewell that ought to have been private.

Before Blade could move, Neena rose and turned to him. Her arms were still raised, but now they reached out toward him, beckoning him to come closer. As though pulled by invisible strings, Blade did so.

He came within Neena's reach, and her arms went around him. Her body swayed forward and pressed hard against his.

She had embraced him and he had embraced her before, many times. It had always been an embrace that a sister might have given a brother, or a brother a sister. This time it was different. Weeks of captivity, weeks of endurance, the tension and violence of their escape, their trek through the forests of Gleor—bit by bit, all these things had forged a bond between Blade and Neena. Now they had the time, the place, and the strength to complete that bond.

Neena's hands crept down and around, to stroke the inside of Blade's thighs. His own hands slipped to the front of her tunic and began undoing the lacing. The leather opened; his fingers crept inside and slid around the superb curves of her small neat breasts, over her suddenly firm nipples. Neena's lips quivered, drifted open, pressed warmly and wetly against Blade's.

Blade finished undoing the lacing of her tunic and pulled it from her body. Now she was bare to the waist. He bent down, his lips joining his hands in roaming up and down her body, over throat, shoulders, breasts, the

85

smooth, flat stomach. He kissed each nipple, felt them harden still further against his searching lips, heard Neena moan softly, deep in her throat.

He would have started on the lacing of her trousers then, but her hands got there first. She pushed her trousers down her long slim legs. They wadded and tangled around her ankles and caught on her boots. She pushed and shoved and heaved at them, half cursing, half laughing in frustration and passion and impatience all mixed together. Finally she threw herself on her back, arms spread wide, hair fanning out on the grass. She could raise her legs, but she could not spread them. They were locked together at the ankles by her tangled trousers as effectively as they had been by Lord Desgo's hobbling cords. She kicked furiously, tried to sit up, then fell over backward and lay there choking and gasping with laughter until she was too weak to even raise her head.

Blade stripped off his own loincloth and stood naked in the sunlight, staring down at Neena. Her eyes widened as she took in the whole magnificent maleness of his powerful body. He knelt, jerked off her boots with two swift motions that made her gasp, then slid her trousers off and threw them aside. Now her legs could slide apart in a single fluid motion.

In another equally fluid motion Blade was balancing himself on his arms above her. Neena's lips moved in wordless demands that he enter her, that they join. He held himself above her for another moment, until her hands reached up and grabbed his hair and beard. She jerked his head downward so hard that for another moment sharp pain almost drove away his desire.

Easily Blade lowered himself, gently but firmly he entered Neena. Her eyes widened until Blade could see the whites, then flickered shut. Her mouth opened in another, very different sort of gasp, then hungrily sought his again.

She was silent for a little while after that, but her body spoke more than loud enough. Her lips devoured his, her arms went around him and her nails raked up and down his back, her legs clamped tightly around him. She gripped him tightly in every way she could manage, by

86

everything she could reach or touch or take into herself. She seemed to be afraid that if she loosened any part of her grip for a single moment, Blade would float away and their joining would be incomplete.

Blade wasn't going anywhere. He would have gripped Neena as tightly as she was gripping him if he hadn't been afraid of what his own strength might do to to her. He seldom felt a woman throwing herself into the act of love as Neena was doing. He seldom felt as completely drawn into it himself. All his awareness and every breath he took were centered on the woman he held and who held him.

He felt her beginning to twist back and forth under him as he rose and fell inside her. He felt blood joining the sweat where her nails clawed at his back. He heard her gasp, then sob out loud, then begin a low, continuous moaning. The moan grew steadily louder. As it rose, so did Blade's own passion. He was gasping now, trying desperately to hold on, hold back, carry through to the end.

Neena's moan turned into a shriek that echoed around the clearing, sending birds and animals squawking and whirring and crashing away in all directions. She arched upward against Blade as he pressed down into her, clawed, bit, sobbed, gasped, tossed her head from side to side so that her hair fell like a blanket over both of them.

Before Neena's climax could pass, Blade reached his. He did not shout, because all the breath seemed to go out of his body in a great sigh along with his hot jetting into Neena. He clamped his arms around her, and for a moment he held back none of his strength. She did not protest, she did not care, she hardly seemed to notice. In that moment he could have crushed half her bones to powder and it would have been several minutes before she noticed what had happened.

Those several minutes passed, as they lay locked and tangled together in the flattened grass, sweat trickling off them and the sun beating down on them. Eventually their breathing slowed until they could hear the world around them, and their vision cleared until they could see it. It was more minutes before either of them could move or

87

speak. Then they sat up, brushed themselves off, and looked at each other.

Blade noticed that barely ten feet off to one side of them was where Kubona's body had lain. Twenty feet to the other side lay the skeleton of one of Desgo's soldiers. Neena saw where he was looking, and laughed.

"No, Blade, I doubt we need fear that their spirits will have anything to say about what we have done here. Kubona—well, she was no more a blushing virgin than I. If she watched us, she will go happily and in peace, seeing our happiness."

"And the soldiers' spirits?"

"If they were still around to watch—well, they have seen us alive and happy. *They* will go off to torment, knowing that they died in vain, that we returned here together, to love in the very place where they died. I doubt if we could have found a better way of adding to their torments."

Blade laughed at Neena's ferocity. Then he said, more seriously, "I think we would do well to get our clothes on and get back to camp."

"You would rather hide in the darkness than lie in the sun?"

"I would rather spend the rest of the day where no one can see us. There *may* be only the spirits of Trawn's soldiers left in these woods. I would rather not find out otherwise when a spear drives through your guts."

Neena sighed, then nodded. Together they rose and pulled on their clothes. Then hand in hand they slipped back into the forest.

Chapter 15

By the time they got back to the camp in the hollow tree, Neena was ready to make love again. They lay down in the musty darkness among the dried vines and leaves and joined once more. After that Neena seemed contented at last, and slowly drifted off to sleep with a smile on her face. Blade lay quietly beside her for a while. Eventually he was able to ignore the rumblings of his half-empty stomach and join Neena in sleep.

They slept through the rest of the day and most of the night. In the gray light before dawn Blade awoke to find Neena already up and rummaging through the gear. As he watched, she gave a little cry of triumph, and drew out of one bag a wide golden bracelet. It was studded with enormous emeralds that blazed with a magnificent cold green fire even in the semidarkness.

"Blade, raise your left arm."

There was a note in Neena's voice that Blade had never heard before. It was unmistakably a note of command, but at the same time surprisingly gentle. Blade obeyed.

Neena snapped the bracelet open, put it around Blade's left wrist, and snapped it shut again. She let his arm drop, then rocked backward, kneeling naked before him. Her eyes fixed themselves intently on Blade's face.

"Now, by the will of the gods, by the laws and customs of Draad, and most important of all, by my choice, you are betrothed husband to me, Neena, Princess of Draad."

Blade hadn't seen this coming, but he wasn't particularly surprised, and not at all unhappy about it. To be betrothed to a woman of high rank would give him a place in Draad that might prove valuable. To be betrothed to Neena, with her beauty, skill, and lively wit, would be far more than useful. It would be a very agreeable experience indeed.

His ruby ring that he'd snatched back from Lord Desgo was on his finger. Slowly he took it off.

"Neena, it is your turn. Hold out your left hand."

Blade took the small, strong hand and thrust the ring on to the index finger. It was too large to stay on any of the others. He smiled as Neena raised her hand to look at the ring, then spoke.

"Now, by the will of the gods, the laws and customs of England, and by my consent, you are betrothed wife to me, Blade, Prince of England."

To his surprise he saw tears glimmering in Neena's eyes. He said nothing, only reached out and brushed one hand lightly across her cheeks, brushing away the tears.

"I am happy, Neena," he said.

"So am I," she said, her voice not quite steady. "My father—well, whether he is happy or not, I doubt he will say anything against you. He has long known that I would have no husband except one I chose for myself. I have chosen you, and as he loves me, I think he will not let himself hate you."

That was just as well with Blade. He had no objection to marrying Neena. He would, however, rather not make an enemy of King Embor by doing so.

"In fact," she went on, "I think he may find good reason to be happier with you than with any man of Draad. Any of the warriors or chiefs' sons I might otherwise have chosen would be of one clan or another. The clan of my husband would rejoice. The others would not, and some of them might raise their voices or even their spears against my father. This is not the time for the feuding of the clans of Draad, not when Trawn may march against us at any time.

"Queen Sanaya will be another matter. She will be—"

Neena broke off, looking worried about having perhaps said too much.

Blade placed a finger under her chin and tipped her head up until their eyes met. "Neena, I cannot be all that you will want and need in a husband if you do not tell me what dangers may face me in Draad. You have said enough about Queen Sanaya to make me wonder about her. I have met such women as her before, and they have seldom been my friends."

"You see clearly, Blade," said Neena. "You also speak the truth. I shall tell you of her, although it may seem almost too simple. Sanaya knows that if I take a husband, I may soon bear a son to him. Then she will no longer be the only bearer of sons to the royal house of Draad. Her position will be weakened, and if she angers my father as she has done in the past, he may not again hold back from setting her aside."

"I see."

"You do not see everything. If Sanaya fears this, she will be desperate, and when she is desperate, she becomes dangerous. She will be dangerous to both of us, but she will concentrate on you."

Blade nodded. "I shall be on the alert."

"You certainly should be. I do not know how far Sanaya may go to defend herself. You should also take care for your own desires. Sanaya is extremely beautiful, and is said to be experienced and skilled as well. I would take it much amiss if you were to bed her."

Blade nodded again. He was tempted to ask Neena exactly what she would do to him if she "took amiss" something that he did. He decided it might not be wise, and instead changed the subject.

"Do you find the ring beautiful?"

"Yes. There is no such stone in all the forests of Gleor or the earth below them."

"It is a magical stone from my home land, called a ruby. I have given it to you to signal our betrothal, but I fear I must ask for it back when we reach Draad."

Neena looked sulky, almost like a small girl. "Why?"

"As I said, it is a magical stone, that can receive spells. A great Kaireen and sorcerer of my people, named Lord Leighton, filled that stone with protective spells. I will be in danger, from Sanaya and many other people, if I do not wear it after we return to Draad." Blade wondered what Lord Leighton would say to being described as a "sorcerer." The scientist would probably throw at least a small fit.

Neena sighed and shrugged. "Very well, I shall not leave you without protection. But I shall wear the ruby until we reach Draad, and that will be more than a week."

They gathered up their clothing, gear, and weapons, and moved out. By the time the sun rose over the forest, they were well on the march toward the east.

That afternoon they hunted. Neena brought down a pair of apelike creatures covered with brown fur, while Blade speared a large snake. Behind a screen of bushes

91

along the bank of a swift-flowing stream, they built a fire of driftwood and twigs and roasted their catch. By the time they were through, there was nothing left of either the apes or the snake but the entrails and bones sucked clean before being tossed aside.

Blade sighed contentedly, wiped his hands and mouth with a bunch of leaves, and leaned back against a tree trunk.

"Our forests can provide well, can they not?" said Neena.

Blade smiled. "They can. Of course, I think the snake should really have been allowed to hang for three days, then been marinated for twenty-four hours in a sauce of red wine, leeks, thyme, and—" That was as far as he got before Neena burst out laughing, then put both hands on his chest and shoved him over backward. Before he could rise she was swarming all over him, and they did not get up for quite a while after that.

It took them nearly a week to reach the nearest of the villages of Draad. The forests spread thickly across the land, but there was plenty of water, game, and fruit, and there was little danger of meeting any hunters or raiders from Trawn. Neena hoped they might meet a hunting party from Draad, but luck was not with them there. Even without that last piece of luck, Blade found the march to Draad as pleasant as a camping trip, at least compared with everything that had gone before it.

They spent two days climbing steadily higher. The forest grew thinner, the swarming insects faded away, the nights were almost chilly, and beyond the treetops Blade caught glimpses of mist-shrouded mountains.

"The Mountains of Hoga," said Neena. "They are a great barrier to the raiders of Trawn. With the mountain clans, they have done much to keep our land free so far. I fear, though, that what has been enough in the past will not be enough before much longer."

At a place Neena called the Pass of Mezan, they met the first of the mountain clansmen. Blade could see that they were of the same stock as Neena. All were tall, slim but superbly muscled, with pale brown skins and hair so black that it showed blue tints in the sunlight. Both men and women appeared carrying weapons, which was the way among the mountain clans. It was not the way elsewhere in Draad.

"If things elsewhere in Draad were done as wisely and as well as among the mountain clans, we would be in far less danger," said Neena bitterly. "They turn out everyone who can fight, they know their land, they spend little time fighting or intriguing among themselves."

Things beyond the Mountains of Hoga were rather different, or so Blade gathered. King Embor was hardly a king so much as he was referee for the squabbling and feuding of a score of clans, each with their own cluster of lands and villages. The fact that they were outnumbered three or four to one by the warriors of Trawn and their stolofs had so far done nothing to unite all the petty rulers in Draad.

"This has not as yet been fatal," said Neena. "The mountain people can fight off any small raiding parties from Trawn. The kings of Trawn have only once sent a large army all the way to our borders, and that was centuries ago, before the time of the stolofs. Now, though, if they come, they will come with the stolofs, and for us—" Neena sighed, in her weariness and her fear for her people.

The mountain clans had heard that Neena was missing, and her father much grieved over it. They rejoiced in a rather sober fashion over her return, throwing a feast with masses of roast meat, koba nuts, fish from the mountain streams, and a sour but strong nut beer.

Neena asked the chiefs not to send messengers on to her father. Impishly, she wanted her safe return home to be a surprise.

The clansmen must have ignored her wishes. Two days beyond the Mountains of Hoga, Blade and Neena were approaching the first of the lowland villages. It was there that they met King Embor, with all his court, all his guard of warriors—and all his problems.

Chapter 16

Neena pointed out her father to Blade as soon as the king came in sight. Blade would not have needed her help. It was obvious at once who among the people facing them was King Embor of Draad.

Embor was half a head taller than Blade, but like his daughter he was slim and fine boned. The loss of flesh that comes with age had turned his slimness almost into gauntness, but his movements were sure and fluid and graceful. He carried himself with a dignity that Blade would have called "regal" even if Embor hadn't been a king.

The king's skin was the same color as his daughter's, but his dark hair and small square beard had turned a gray that was already shading into silver. He wore a necklace of gold links holding together copper disks set with large emeralds, emerald rings on four fingers, and a sword with a truly enormous emerald set in the hilt. He wore a tunic and trousers of monkey fur dyed red, soft leather boots, and a copper-studded belt, but no crown.

Embor stepped forward toward Blade and Neena, and the warriors with him gave way to either side. Most of them were looking intently at Blade, and several had their spears raised. One went so far as to nock an arrow to his bow and point it at Blade. That drew a glare from King Embor, and the warrior hastily dropped the arrow back in his quiver.

"Well, daughter," said Embor, with a surprisingly gentle smile. He looked at the moment much more the father than the king and warrior. "So you return to us safely—and with a husband." Then his reserve broke down completely, and he stepped forward and embraced his daughter. For a long moment they stood, holding each other. The warriors smiled broadly.

One person in the group was not smiling, at least not

94

while King Embor's attention was all on his daughter. This was a tall woman, large boned and almost voluptuous, her perfectly molded face framed in a mass of mahogany-colored hair. She also wore garments of red-dyed monkey fur and a necklace of gold, copper, and emeralds. For all her beauty, though, her face was chill and blank, except when her eyes fell on Neena. Then unmistakable hatred flashed in them.

Blade did not try to meet the woman's eyes or attract her attention. He knew who she was without being told—Queen Sanaya. What he saw in her eyes also confirmed everything Neena had said about the queen's being an enemy. Very well, he would accept that—then wait for her to make the first move. Sanaya was queen of Draad, and he was a newcomer. How strong his position as Neena's husband would be, he couldn't be sure. He did not want to put the matter to a test out of sheer carelessness.

Eventually Embor and Neena unwound from each other. The king turned to Blade. "You come here as the betrothed husband of my daughter, so I will not ask many questions that I would ask otherwise. I do not despise her judgment enough to believe that she would choose one unworthy, and LET NO ONE ELSE DO SO EITHER!" His voice boomed out suddenly, and Queen Sanaya jumped like a startled horse.

"So be it," he said, stepping forward with both hands outstretched. Blade stretched out his own hands and the king took them. "There is much I do not know of you and what you and my daughter have done to escape from Trawn. I shall ask you and Neena to tell me all of it, at another time and in another place. Here and now, I say only—be welcome in Draad, my son."

Embor embraced Blade. Over the king's shoulder Blade could see both Neena and Sanaya. They were alternately glaring at each other and watching Embor and Blade. Neena's face was split in a broad grin as she saw her father embrace her husband. Sanaya's face was frozen again, so completely that not even her eyes gave any clues to the emotions that were certainly bubbling inside her.

With Blade and Neena joined to it, the royal party turned about and headed back down into the valley of Draad. Everyone marched except Queen Sanaya and an elderly man Neena described as the High Kaireen, the most important scholar in Draad. These two were carried in litters. Everyone else walked, from King Embor down to the thirty-odd servants with the party.

They walked fast, too. At the end of each day's march Blade was quite happy to sink down onto the ground beside the king's campfire, drink beer from wooden cups, and tell King Embor of his and Neena's adventures in Trawn.

As King Embor learned more of what had happened to Blade and Neena, Blade learned more about Draad. Much merely confirmed what he'd already heard from Neena—the prickly rivalry of the clans, King Embor as a referee, the skill and endurance of the hunters and warriors of Draad in the great forests.

Other things were new. Neena had not told him that Draad was poor in metals, for example. Only the greatest chiefs and warriors could afford swords. Everyone else had to make do with spears and arrows or clubs and axes with stone heads. These served well enough for hunting. Facing the swordsmen and the stolofs of Trawn was another matter.

Of the metals, iron was fairly common, and the Kaireens and their servants had some skill in working it. Copper, on the other hand, was so rare that only the highest in the land could afford to wear a few disks of it as jewelry. The copper in King Embor's great royal necklace was worth more than half a dozen large rich villages with all their people, beasts, and land.

On the other hand, the people of Draad had a good many skills and resources that helped make up for their lack of metals. There were the emeralds, which *poured* out of rich mines in the southern part of the great valley. There was also the threebo tree. This bamboolike plant had round jointed stalks that could be cut into tough spear shafts, axe handles, and eight-foot quarterstaffs that were called threebos after the tree itself.

Blade made a notable impression on the warriors of King Embor's guard by defeating half a dozen of them in quick succession in bouts with the threebo. Then King Embor challenged him. He could have defeated the king as well, but managed to avoid doing so without being detected at it. King Embor would probably not object to being defeated by his new son-in-law. But the king had too many enemies who might draw the wrong conclusions from such a defeat.

There were also leaves, resins, and barks that the people of Draad had learned to use with great skill. They also had a surprisingly advanced medical science, which Blade saw in action one day.

The royal party was marching on a wide path along the shore of a lake. It was a gray, damp morning with the lake's surface as smooth as glass. Suddenly a woman burst out of the bushes toward the lake, waving her arms and screaming.

"Lord, oh lord king, send a Kaireen! Send one, send! My son, my son, a black stalker has him! A Kaireen, for the love of the gods!"

The royal party scurried into action. King Embor summoned six warriors of his guard. The High Kaireen climbed out of his litter, summoned his assistants, and lined up with the warriors. A chance to practice his medical skills seemed to have taken twenty years off his age.

"May I go with them, Lord?" said Blade.

"Certainly," said Embor. "The arts of our Kaireens are no secret."

Blade fell in with the rescue party and marched off with it as the woman led it down toward the lake shore. As they marched, the woman calmed down enough to give a more coherent explanation of what had happened. Apparently the black stalker—some sort of large carnivorous animal—hadn't actually carried off her son. But it had mangled his leg rather gruesomely.

They found the boy soon enough. He was lying on the grass beside a log hut near the shore of the lake. His right leg seemed to have been hacked from thigh to ankle with

97

razor-sharp axes. He was unconscious and deathly pale, but still breathing regularly.

The High Kaireen took one look, then turned to his assistants. "The leg must come off." The mother whimpered and sank to her knees beside her son. "Forgive me, little mother, but there is no choice if your son is to live. The leg will never hold him up again. Instead it will fester and burn, and in the end finish what the black stalker began." The woman turned blank eyes on the old man, then nodded slowly.

The assistants went rapidly to work. One of them drew out a saw, with iron teeth set in a wooden bar. The other drew out a stained pad of cloth and a leather bottle. He removed a wooden stopper from the bottle and poured several ounces of the liquid on the cloth. Finally he gripped the boy's hair with one hand and clamped the soaked cloth over his nose and mouth with the other.

The boy mewled and writhed. The High Kaireen had to hold his shoulders before he would stay still. Even then it was a long time before his breathing became regular as he slipped down into unconsciousness.

Once the anesthetic took effect, the assistants went swiftly to work. Both seemed to be competent surgeons. In a matter of minutes they had the mangled leg off and the stump bound up and bandaged. They seemed to have some hints of antiseptic principles—they were careful to keep their hands clean, and did not let the wound or the bandages touch the ground.

Blade had a host of questions he wanted to ask about medicine in Draad, and particularly the anesthetic liquid. It occurred to him, however, that showing *too* much curiosity could arouse suspicions and make him enemies. He kept quiet while the High Kaireen carefully explained to the woman how to take care of her son, and how another trained man would be sent from the nearest village in a few days. The woman kept nodding without saying anything. Blade hoped she understood at least half of the excellent advice she was getting. The High Kaireen obviously knew a good deal more about medicine than Blade would have expected from even the most learned man among such a primitive people.

They were on the way back to join the rest of the party before the High Kaireen felt like speaking. "Prince Blade," he said. "You watched with interest my people at work. There are Kaireens in your land of England?"

"Yes, quite a few."

"Are they wiser than I?"

Blade sensed that the old man was asking to be praised, although he did not seem like the sort to appreciate really gross flattery.

"Some are," said Blade. "A great many are not." That was both flattering and accurate. The High Kaireen seemed to be a man able to use all of his intelligence for any purpose that interested him. That made him a wise man by any standards of any dimension.

The High Kaireen smiled graciously. "Thank you. I do not imagine, then, that our skills have many surprises for you."

This was an admirable opening. Blade shrugged. "Not many. But the liquid you poured on the cloth—the one that made the boy sleep—that interests me. I—"

"That?" The High Kaireen sighed wearily. "The sleeping water from the peza leaves? It is a strange jest of the gods."

"How is this? It saved that boy much pain."

"Yes, it is better to have it than not to have it at all. But it is not all that good. It is made by boiling peza leaves in water from mountain springs, then letting the liquid settle. When it has settled one takes the part close to the bottom, and that is the sleeping water. It is not strong enough, for as you saw even a small weak boy took a long time to fall asleep. Yet if one uses too much, it is very easy for the sleep to turn into death."

"You have no way of making it stronger?"

"The gods have given us no such knowledge, Blade, not in all the years we have been using the sleeping water. I suppose they will never give it to us. Perhaps they wish us to endure pain, to remind us that we are weak after all."

99

"Perhaps," said Blade. His mind was no longer entirely on his conversation with the High Kaireen. Instead, part of it was drawing conclusions from what the old man said and leaping on ahead to exciting guesses.

The anesthetic was too weak and too unreliable. That was not surprising, considering the crude methods used in making it. Suppose one developed a way of *distilling* the sleeping water, so that it was five, six, ten times as powerful?

Yes, but distillation involved metal tubing, large quantities of it. There wasn't enough copper in all of Draad to make a single good still. Nor was there the skill in iron working needed to make usable pipes out of iron.

True enough, all of it. But threebo stalks are hollow, and the wood is strong, tough, and waterproof. Seal the joints with resins and leaves, and you might have exactly what you need for a still. It would be a weird-looking setup, all the tubing probably zigzagging instead of coiled. But it might work. If it worked, Draad's sick and wounded would have cause to bless the name of Prince Blade for a long time to come.

Blade smiled at the thought. Then his mind took another leap ahead, and abruptly his face straightened out. Suppose you could make the sleeping water even stronger than you needed for an anesthetic? Then you'd have something usable as a weapon. Spray a good dose of it on a man, and he'd go down.

A man—or a stolof. A man might be fast enough on his feet to evade the spray. But a stolof? They were deadly, true, but they were not that fast on their eight feet. Attacked by brave men spraying powerful sleeping water, what would happen to them? They might be knocked out. Certainly they would be far too slow to fight, to kill, to hurl their deadly ribbons with such accuracy.

Blade swallowed. For a moment he felt almost dizzy at the possibilities opening up in front of him. He felt as though he was slightly drunk and standing on top of a high cliff in the darkness, with a strong cold wind blowing around him.

The sensation faded, and Blade began to think clearly

100

again. There were a hundred questions he'd have to answer before he could say if his idea made sense or not. How did stolofs breathe? How well could the joints of threebos be sealed? What with? And so on.

Well, he would just have to go about finding out the answers. In the meantime he would keep his mouth shut. He did not want to arouse vain hopes in those who would be his friends. He also did not want to arouse jealousy and all the things that might follow from jealousy in those people who could easily become his enemies.

Neena came out to greet him as he approached the main party. "Blade, you look—strange. As though something very important had happened to you."

"I do?" He shook his head. "I did not know. I suppose it is just being happy that we have saved the boy. That is all that has happened, and isn't that enough?" Even Neena would have to remain ignorant for the time being.

"I suppose so," she said, and took his arm.

Chapter 17

Draad had no real capital city. Instead there was a cluster of a dozen or so large villages that King Embor ruled directly. Their hunters and warriors provided his guard, and their crops and animals supplied his table. Embor himself lived in a log-walled compound hardly larger than that of one of the principal clan chiefs.

Blade was just as happy not to have to live in the middle of a vast palace, with a swarming horde of courtiers and servants to watch everything he did and hear everything he said. He wanted to push his inquiries forward without anyone watching him or eavesdropping on him. In King Embor's home, he could move about freely and quietly, seeing what he wanted to see, asking questions wherever he wanted to, with no one paying any attention.

He had plenty of time to himself. He had high rank and honor, as a warrior, a foreign prince, and above all as Princess Neena's betrothed. But he had no specific duties, or at least none to anyone except Neena. She demanded a vigorous performance of those duties. Yet no matter how demanding she was, she could not take up all of Blade's time. He quickly learned more about turning threebos and sleeping water into weapons. The more he learned, the more optimistic he became.

He finally reached the point of asking to meet with King Embor and the High Kaireen. He also asked Neena to attend the meeting. In fact, he wouldn't have dared not to ask her, even if he hadn't respected her judgment as highly as he did.

Blade sometimes thought it was rather a pity that Neena was from Dimension X, rather than Home Dimension. She seemed to have the perfect balance of physical and mental development needed to make a field agent, one good enough to travel among the dimensions. It was frustrating to know that she could never be tested and trained into what she might so easily become!

The four people met in King Embor's most private chamber, locked away in the innermost part of the great sprawling house. The room was dark except for a pair of flickering candles. The air was close and heavy with the scents of wood, resin, wax, and dry rot.

Blade began with a plain, unadorned statement.

"I have been looking for a way to destroy the stolofs of the army of Trawn. I think I have found that way. Now I need your help to be sure."

That certainly got their attention. All three of them stared at him as if he had just turned into a stolof himself. Then King Embor cleared his throat and nodded.

"Go on, Prince Blade. Tell us more."

Blade did so. He ran over all that he'd guessed and all that he'd learned for certain, about stolofs, sleeping water, threebos, distillation, and everything else that was part of his plan. He had a number of drawings, made with charcoal on bleached parchment. One showed the distillation apparatus. Another showed how four men could attack and slay a stolof. Two would have swords or spears, two would have containers of the distilled sleeping water. King Embor and Neena were particularly interested in that second drawing.

Blade ran through his entire presentation without getting any questions from the other three. He wasn't sure if they understood him perfectly, didn't understand him at all, or were too surprised to say anything either way. When he'd finished, he looked at King Embor. Their eyes met and slowly, like a man waking from sleep, King Embor nodded.

"You have thought deeply and spoken wisely, Prince Blade. Are the warriors of England also trained as Kaireens?"

"We are given some of their learning, as are your warriors here in Draad. But I would not presume to claim for myself the high rank of Kaireen. No, I am just a man who has traveled far and remembered much of what he has seen in those travels."

"You have not seen stolofs, though?"

"Not until I came to Gleor, and I am just as happy about that. I do not much care for those beasts!"

Neena laughed. "Every warrior of Draad could say the same. But few have the courage to admit that they are not as brave as they want women to think!" Her eyes caressed Blade.

"In any case," Blade went on, "I have seen many other large and savage beasts. I have also seen some of them made weak and slow moving by breathing sleeping water. I am sure that a weak or slow moving stolof could not last for a moment against the warriors of Draad."

"I hope you are right," said Embor.

The High Kaireen nodded. "I hope we shall have a chance to discover *if* Prince Blade is right," he said gently. "It will take a great deal of work. Much of it Prince Blade will do, but much also must be done by other men. For example, you will need a great quantity of peza leaves, will you not?"

"I shall," said Blade. "Many basketfuls will be needed while I am learning. Then many more while I am making

103

the strong sleeping water. I will also need much help when I begin making large amounts of the water."

"This is certain," said King Embor. "Well, any part of my house is yours to use, and the labor of any man or woman in it is yours to command."

"I have other thoughts on this matter," said the High Kaireen. "With your permission?" looking at the king. Embor nodded.

"Very well. The peza tree grows throughout Draad, but it is truly abundant only in the Mountains of Hoga. To bring the quantities of leaves Blade will need to the royal house from the mountains will take many men many days. They will not be able to do other work, in the forests or the fields or the shops. The leaves themselves will not be fresh, and we do not know what this may do to Blade's sleeping water. Also, if many men are carrying baskets of peza leaves from the Mountains of Hoga to the royal house, people will see them doing this. They will wonder why this is happening, and they will ask questions. Sooner or later they will learn what is going on. Do we wish this?"

King Embor shook his head.

"We do not wish very many people to know what Prince Blade is doing. There are few of our people so wicked that they would steal the secret and sell it to Trawn—"

"That's nice to say, father," put in Neena. "But I don't believe it. I don't think you do either."

"Keep your silence for the moment, daughter," said Embor, with a weary smile. "The gods give you better luck in keeping this girl silent than I have had, Prince Blade."

Neena stuck out her tongue at Blade, and he grinned at her. "I doubt if the gods will have much to say on the matter," he said. "Neena is as she is, and not much likely to change."

"You see, father," said Neena. "The gods have sent me a wise husband."

"I hope so," said King Embor. "As I was saying, a few of Draad will sell the secret in Trawn. But I can see many

104

stealing it and then claiming that they have discovered it. That will give them much honor, and take away honor from you, Prince Blade."

"Jealous men are dangerous enemies, that is true," said Blade. "What does the High Kaireen propose?"

"There is a house high in the Mountains of Hoga, a strong house with a strong wall around it. It is used by Kaireens and others who wish to spend some time apart from the world, meditating and writing. Around the house peza trees grow so thickly that their fallen leaves cover the ground to the depth of a tall man's knees. If we were to send to that house several assistants, and all the things Blade may ask for, it might be a good place for him to work. He and all that he does will be far away from prying eyes and ears."

"He will also be close to the mountains, where those of Trawn may raid," said Embor.

"You forget the mountain clans," said Neena. "They can send warriors and hunters to stand guard around the house. Those guards will keep their eyes and ears to themselves and their mouths shut. They are better servants than most of the lowland clans, father."

"Neena, pray cease to tell me my business," said Embor wearily. He gave the impression of having been over this same ground with his daughter many times before. Blade found it hard to keep from smiling.

"The High Kaireen's proposal seems wise to me," said Blade. "We must not let ambitious men or traitors get hold of the secret of the new sleeping water. The first that those of Trawn learn of it must be the day we strike down their stolofs by the hundred!"

"To hundreds of dead stolofs!" Neena raised her beer cup in a toast, and the other three all drank with her.

As Blade and Neena walked back to their private chambers, Neena took Blade's arm firmly. Her grip was so tight that her nails dug into his flesh.

"Do you run off into the Mountains of Hoga to run away from me, or perhaps to some mountain woman?"

She was grinning, but Blade was not entirely sure that

she was joking. Fortunately he had an honest answer ready for her.

"I seek no other woman than you, Neena. I need none, and do not see how I could."

"Good. As long as it is that way, you and I shall live in peace. Otherwise I will be angry." Blade did not feel like asking what she might do to him if she did become angry.

Chapter 18

The house that the High Kaireen gave Blade lay high up in the Mountains of Hoga, lonely and isolated. Only a few miles to the west was the tree line. Beyond the trees Blade could see bare peaks of gray and blue rock and even the white glinting of snowcaps.

He could seldom see that far, though. Two days out of three, gray mist or grayer clouds surrounded him. Then the house seemed to be alone in an otherwise empty world.

The days were often cool and the nights usually chilly. Blade did not notice this. He spent all the hours of the day and a good part of the night in his steaming hot workshop. Fires burned there around the clock, under bubbling pots of resin or boiling cauldrons of leaves. Smoke and steam rose up in clouds and swirled around Blade. Sometimes they found a way out through the crude chimney or the cracks in the boarded-up windows. Most of the time they didn't.

Blade set himself a grueling pace as he assembled and tested the distilling apparatus. That took several weeks. He had been right in theory. With threebo stems, resin, and iron or stone pots one could put together a fairly serviceable piece of equipment. Putting that theory into practice took time and effort, much of both wasted. Finally Blade managed to build something that would neither leak nor explode nor catch fire, and he was able to really go to work.

He now worked harder than ever, sixteen and eighteen hours a day. At the end of the day he was frequently exhausted or dizzy and only half-awake from the sleeping water's steam. He could do nothing except stagger to his sleeping room and collapse.

Blade grew lean and hungry looking, his eyes were perpetually red and inflamed, his hands were callused, black with caked soot and sticky with resin. It was probably a good thing that Neena wasn't with him. He would hardly have time to kiss her goodnight!

The High Kaireen gave Blade four carefully chosen assistants. All of them were strong young men, none of them stupid and all of them good at taking orders.

"They were chosen for those qualities," the High Kaireen told Blade. "Their orders are to do as you tell them, keep you and the house and everything in it from harm, and otherwise keep their mouths shut."

"What about the guards to be sent by the mountain clans?"

"They will never come within the walls around the house. Nor will they know what you do within, except that you work to do much harm to those of Trawn. That is enough to make sure that the mountain people will keep their mouths closed and their vigil unbroken. They hate those of Trawn in a way you would not understand unless you had spent years among them."

The four assistants obeyed their orders, as far as Blade could tell. They never objected to working a fifteen-hour day, seldom spoke unless spoken to, and seemed to be able to live without food or sleep. He had no idea of how much they were learning about what he was doing, or how much they would be able to tell anyone else about it. Even if they knew all of his secrets, they would find it hard to get through the mountain clansmen and reach anyone who would listen to them.

The clansmen were also obeying their orders. Blade never saw them from the house during the day. Occasionally he would hear soft footfalls and see shadowy human figures moving past with feline grace in the darkness. At other times he would be out in the woods, supervising the gathering of a fresh batch of peza leaves. Suddenly the assistants would start, and sometimes drop their baskets, as two or three fur-clad figures slipped out from behind the bushes. The mountain people never stopped to talk and barely stopped to look. A moment, and they would be gone into the dripping forest as silently as they had come. At times Blade had the feeling that his laboratory was guarded by an endless coming and going of ghosts or spirits.

The youngest of the four assistants, named Kulo, turned out to have a positive genius for woodcarving. This became more and more useful as Blade's work demanded more and more precisely made equipment. Blade set Kulo some nearly impossible tasks, but somehow the young man always rose to the occasion.

That was encouraging to Blade. It would soon be time to make the first of the weapons designed for use with the distilled sleeping water. He was now spending hours with charcoal and parchment, making rough sketches of various ideas. If they could not be turned into usable weapons, all his work here would be wasted.

That was one of the thoughts that always drove Blade back to his workshop. Sometimes it made him wish that there were more than twenty-four hours in a day.

One gray morning, things were going so well in the workshop that Blade slept late and ate a leisurely breakfast. Then he went out to help bring in a caravan of porters bringing more threebo stems. Although the threebo grew this high in the mountains, it grew more abundantly in the lowlands, and the warmer weather down there made the stems grow thicker and stronger. So the High Kaireen sent eight porter loads of threebo wood up to Blade each week.

Blade met the caravan half a mile downhill from the workshop. He saw the porters plod up the path toward him, each man with a bundle of threebo wood strapped across his shoulders. Blade stood while they passed by, sweating in spite of the coolness of the morning, carefully

108

seeking out footholds in the damp earth under their feet. Not for the first time, Blade wished he could tell the people helping him at least some of what he was trying to do. That might make all the sweat and all the long hours seem more worthwhile. But the secret had to remain a secret for a while longer.

Of course Kulo had probably already guessed much of what Blade planned. But Kulo was also the one Blade trusted most, in spite of his youth. Kulo would keep his mouth shut.

Blade watched the last of the porters disappear up the hill into the dripping forest. For the moment he was alone among the trees, and he savored the sensation. He had been busy too long, with too many hours spent in smoke and fume-laden air in the dark, almost airless workshop. The limitless forests of Gleor in all their wild beauty were all around him; he should take more advantage of this.

After the work is over, he told himself firmly. After he had found his answer to the stolofs, he and Neena would come back up here for a few days by themselves. Then there would be time to hunt, bathe in the mountain streams (as cold as they were), make love in—

A soft whistle sounded behind Blade. He turned around, drawing his sword as he did so.

One of the mountain hunters stood beside a huge moss-grown tree, raising a hand in salute to Blade.

"Hail, Prince Blade. One of my brothers has been bitten by a snake. He has need of a Kaireen's wisdom to heal him. We have heard that you have that wisdom, along with your warrior's skills. Will you follow me, and do what can be done to aid my brother?"

Blade didn't recognize the man facing him, of course. That was no surprise. He had seen only a handful of clansmen by daylight, and none for very long. The whole thing seemed safe enough, and he did have sword, knife, bow, and arrows. For all the guards in the forest around him, Blade never went anywhere unarmed.

He followed the hunter off into the forest. They went downhill for about a mile, then struck north. The hunter

109

seemed to know exactly where he was going, and set a fast pace. Several times the path led down into hollows that were filled with mist like thick dirty cotton wool. With the trees and the dampness and mist all around, there was little noise except water dripping and their own feet on the path. Even these sounds were weirdly distorted. Almost anyone except Blade would have begun to feel slightly uncomfortable, this far out in an unknown part of the mist-shrouded forest. Even Blade kept his hand close to his sword hilt and his eyes continuously roving about him, searching the forest on all sides.

The hunter led him onward for nearly half an hour. Then suddenly they were in a small clearing. To Blade's right stood a sagging log hut, with a roof of raggedly piled branches. As Blade turned to look more closely at it, the hunter suddenly darted to the left. Before Blade could move or speak, the man vanished into the forest. A moment later even the thud of his running feet faded away, and Blade was alone.

For a moment he was more surprised than angry. Then the thought flashed through his mind that the trees around the clearing could easily conceal an ambush forty men strong.

If there were, then they would most likely be expecting him to turn and run. So he would not do what they expected. Instead of spinning around and dashing off down the path, he dove for the cover of the hut. He would not dive inside, either. Then they could come at him without being seen and burn him out.

Blade flattened himself in the bushes growing up along one side of the hut. He now had cover in one direction and could see in the other three, while he himself was well hidden as long as he kept low. He would do just that, until whoever might be lurking out there made their next move.

Instead, the next move came from inside the hut. Blade heard footsteps, then a low but unmistakably feminine laugh. Still keeping low, Blade crept around toward where he could look into the hut. He had just reached the corner

110

of the hut, when the reed curtain across the door was thrust aside from within.

Queen Sanaya of Draad stepped out into the clearing, threw her head back, and laughed again.

Chapter 19

Blade's first instinct was to go on crouching in the bushes, waiting for the warriors lying in wait in the forest to make their move or for Queen Sanaya to laugh herself into a fit. She was barefoot and wore a flowing blue robe held by an emerald clasp at the throat. Her laughter was low and bubbling, but it somehow echoed around the clearing, and it had a note in it that was not altogether sane.

But Queen Sanaya appeared to know that he—or someone—was close at hand. It would be dangerous to lie here until the queen's unreliable temper broke. It would be less dangerous to rise to his feet and confront her.

Blade thrust his sword back into its sheath and slowly rose to his feet. He kept his arms well out from his side and his fingers spread, to avoid alarming either the queen or some nervous archer or spearman.

Queen Sanaya turned as Blade rose. Her laughter cut off as abruptly as if someone had gripped her by the throat. Her eyes widened. She might have seemed surprised or even frightened, except that her mouth curved into a broad, almost smugly triumphant smile.

"So, Prince Blade," she said. "You came forth into the woods."

"I came forth to where I thought I was needed," said Blade, correcting her in a carefully neutral tone of voice.

"You are a sentimental man."

"There are two opinions about that, here as in most lands—my Lady Queen." Blade was tempted to leave out her title, but that would be too crude and deliberate a slight. He wanted her to go on talking.

111

Sanaya shrugged. "What does one more or less of those dirty mountain men matter to you?"

"It is enough to say that he does matter," said Blade. "I would rather not spend further time arguing the point with you, if there *is* a man who needs aid."

Queen Sanaya laughed again. It was actually more of a low chuckle, and once again Blade had the sense of something not quite sane lurking behind Sanaya's beauty and smiles.

"Then I take it that there is indeed no one who was bitten by a snake?"

"Take what you will, Prince Blade. You seem to be that sort of man."

Blade looked around the clearing, seeking any signs of either wounded men or lurking warriors. He found no sign of the first, but there were six or seven of the latter. The warriors of Gleor were good woodsmen and skilled at concealing themselves. Blade's eyes were even more skilled at picking men out of any sort of concealment.

Queen Sanaya's presence was still a mystery. From all that Blade knew of her, she was fond of her comforts. She would not be tramping about the forests like this merely to act as bait in an ambush by Blade's enemies. It was a mystery he needed to solve.

"Well, I see no man bitten by a snake," he said. "But I think I see a snake here in the clearing."

Queen Sanaya's face hardened. "That may be so."

"It is so. And I think it is a snake that has bitten a good many men so badly that no Kaireen's skill could hope to save them."

"You have strange fancies, Blade."

"Is it certain that they are stranger than yours? You come forth from a perfumed bed in the warm house of the king to these cold damp forests. You draw me into the forests by a lie. You have indeed strange fancies, if you expect to accomplish anything at all by this."

"Indeed?"

"Yes. And do not pull out that toy dagger from your belt and wave it at me. That will accomplish least of all."

112

"You might be surprised, Blade. There may be no serpent here, but there is the power of a serpent's tooth."

Blade took that to mean that the dagger was poisoned. Well, that was about what he might expect of Queen Sanaya.

"Besides," she went on, "you have doubtless noticed those who keep watch. They could do even more than my dagger."

"Perhaps," said Blade. "And again, perhaps not." In a split second he shifted position. Now he stood only inches from the queen, on the side away from her dagger. He was also between her and most of the warriors. "Neither spearmen nor archers can easily strike at me without hitting you. If I were to seize you, what could they do?"

Sanaya's dark eyebrows rose. "Indeed, they will probably not attack. They are good men, among the best I could find. Instead they will watch whatever you do, while some of them run to tell the tale to King Embor and the clan chiefs. What do you imagine they will say and do, when they learn that Prince Blade has attacked the Queen of Draad?"

Blade was perfectly able to imagine what might happen in that case. He had no intention of admitting that to the queen, though.

"Things would be interesting, I am sure."

The queen smiled thinly. "You play your game well, Blade. Your wits are not the dullest of your weapons." She seemed to hesitate for a moment, then licked her lips and said, "Would you like to know how to keep things from becoming—'interesting'?"

"I think, my lady Queen, you will tell me or show me that way, whether I want to learn it or not."

That sharp reply silenced the queen entirely for a moment. Apparently she'd expected a more elegant answer. Elegance be damned! thought Blade. Unless it helped him find out what her game was, he was *not* going to be particularly polite to this royal bitch.

Instead of speaking, Queen Sanaya stepped backward, away from Blade. Then she beckoned him forward. When he was only a couple of feet from her, the queen looked

113

quickly to either side, scanning the bushes and trees around the clearing. Then one hand went to her throat. Her fingers worked at the copper and emerald clasp of her robe, and with a faint click it opened.

Slowly, as though it was caressing her skin as it fell, Sanaya's robe slid down off her shoulders. She let it fall as far as her waist and then caught it with both hands. She stood there, full breasts bare and the nipples already crinkling and hardening as the chill air blew against them. Her eyes were fixed on Blade's face, trying to read his expression.

Blade kept his face expressionless. He wasn't surprised at what the queen had done, even if he hadn't exactly seen it coming. So that was the first part of her plan, was it?

Other parts of his body weren't quite so expressionless. If Sanaya had been able to read them— But she couldn't, at least not yet.

"Well?" said Blade, his voice as cool as he could make it. He suspected the queen was planning to say that word herself, which was why he had used it.

Sanaya was silent for another long moment. Apparently Blade's cool tone was bothering her. Slowly she tied her robe around her waist. Then she brought her hands slowly upward, fingers spread and palms against the smooth, coffee-hued skin of her flat stomach. Her hands rose to cup her breasts. Blade's mind held a moment's vision of his own hands doing the same. The queen's voice was not quite steady when she spoke again.

"Have you hopes, Blade?"

Blade still kept his face straight, although this was becoming more and more of an effort. "Any man has hopes, my Lady Queen."

"Yes, that I know. I also have hopes, though I am but a woman. Help me reach out and grasp those hopes, Prince Blade. Help me." The raw, bubbling desire in her voice was only just under control.

"And if I do not help you?"

Her voice steadied, and for a moment the cold, calculating intriguer looked out of her large dark eyes at Blade.

114

"Then I will run out into the clearing as I am, crying that you have tried to rape me. Many in Draad will not be happy to hear of your lack of control over your desires."

That was a grim certainty. King Embor might or might not forgive Blade for trying to rape his queen and wife. The king was a man of vast patience, but that vast?

Neena would have a fit. Although she might not be driven to violence, she would never let Blade hear the end of the matter. He would no longer be able to rely on her help, advice, and influence.

The clan chiefs and principal warriors would be the worst problem. Too many of them were jealous of Blade's arrival, his new influence, his marriage to Neena. Now they would have a plausible cause. Now they would turn their jealousy into action, and that action against Blade. If he refused Queen Sanaya, he might be dead within a week, and all that he might have done for Draad dead along with him.

What the devil! It was a dilemma he had met before. He had survived and even conquered in spite of the worst wiles of lustful and treacherous women. He would see if he could do the same here again in Draad.

"So be it," he said quietly. "My lady queen, I think your hopes are good ones. Let us step into the hut and talk further of them."

Sanaya's eyes seemed to light up from within with a phosphorescent glow. She swallowed again. "Yes, Blade, let us step into the hut." She turned her back on him and pulled her robe back up to her shoulders with one hand. With the other she pushed aside the curtain across the entrance to the hut. Blade followed her.

Sanaya's robe did not stay on her body very long after the curtain closed behind them. In the mold-scented dark chill of the hut she faced Blade, then let her robe fall again. This time she let it fall all the way to the floor, until it made a crumpled shimmering blue pool around her ankles. Lifting her superb legs, she stepped out of the pool and stood in front of Blade. Except for a small triangle of linen no larger than a handkerchief, she was naked.

Blade was already stripping off his tunic. Sanaya knelt

115

to help him unlace his boots. Her breasts did not sag, but quivered and flowed into new and enticing shapes as she knelt.

Blade kicked off his boots and threw his tunic into a corner of the hut. Before he could do anything else the queen crawled forward on her knees and threw her arms around his waist. Her hair and her lips both brushed lightly, tantalizingly, exquisitely against Blade's skin. He bent slightly and buried his hands in Sanaya's long hair, stroking her temples and the back of her neck as he did so. She nuzzled him harder and moved her lips down his body, to the waist of his trousers.

Then swiftly her hands were at work, unbuckling his belt and unlacing the thongs of the trousers. She pushed the trousers down to his knees and ripped off the breech-clout he wore under them. Blade's aroused and erect maleness greeted her. In turn, she greeted it, her mouth opening wide to take it in, then closing to wrap it in warm, supple lips.

Blade fought back a groan as the warmth and the wetness and the skilled, subtle movements surrounded him. The first moment told him that Sanaya was an un-matched expert at fellatio. The next moment told him that she was determined to match her skill against his endurance, to try driving him to the edge and right over it if she could. He made up his mind that he would use all his own skill and strength to hold back, until Sanaya gave up the struggle and admitted defeat.

So Richard Blade and Sanaya Queen of Draad fought their duel in the dim, damp, chill hut in the forests of Gleor. Sanaya worked her mouth up and down, closed her lips and opened them, licked with her long supple tongue, blew little puffs of air, brought her hands up to stroke and caress what her mouth could not reach. After a while Blade could no longer separate the places where Sanaya was touching him from the places where she wasn't. All his senses seemed focused in his groin, that groin was turning into a white-hot pool, and every nerve in his body seemed to vibrate in time to Sanaya's stroking and sucking.

116

Yet somehow Blade's mind mastered the body that Sanaya was torturing so exquisitely. Somehow he shut away what Sanaya was doing to him in one corner of his awareness. Somehow he held on, until Sanaya's lips began to twist more in a grimace of frustration than anything else. Somehow he held on, until he noticed that Sanaya herself was beginning to sigh and twist from side to side. Her efforts to work Blade up to the point of an erotic explosion were working nearly as well on her.

Blade let Sanaya's mouth take him in once more, deeper than ever, then clamped his hands in her hair again. He held her face against his groin for a moment, then slowly pulled her head back until her eyes were raised to meet his. They did not speak. Blade's throat was too dry and his breath was coming too fast for him to have found words. Sanaya was in much the same shape.

Sanaya nodded, clamped both arms around Blade's waist again, and pulled herself to her feet. Blade pulled his trousers off. Sanaya ripped the small triangle of linen from her body. The hair nestling between her thighs formed a perfect dark triangle, already glistening. She put both hands on Blade's shoulders, and let his hands on her hips draw her hard against him.

They stood pressed hard together for a moment. Blade felt that sweat had already made Sanaya's skin as slick as his own. He could feel the hard solid points of her nipples pressed against his chest as Sanaya's quick breathing thrust her breasts forward.

Then Sanaya let herself sag backward, still holding onto Blade's shoulders with a viselike grip. He had to bend forward to let her keep his grip upon him. She sagged and he bent until she lay back against the floor and he lay down on top of her. She twisted herself into position, raised her legs, bent them double, then clamped one hand in his hair and the other on the back of his neck as he entered her.

In that position she could take him in even more deeply than Blade could have expected. Once again there was warmth and wetness all around him, moving around him, taking him in and sending flames soaring up in his

117

groin. This time he knew he would not be able to last, but it didn't matter now because neither would Sanaya. The duel was over. What they were doing now was more of a duet.

He sensed that the queen felt the same way. At each of Blade's thrusts she would twist and heave herself against him, pressing hard. Less often she would groan, her mouth now open and slack. There was not much tenderness between Blade and Sanaya as they joined. But there was a great deal of passion, and both sensed that passion was rising steadily higher and higher, like water in a well.

It overflowed first in the queen. She gave a terrible cry, as though she were being impaled on something much sharper and more deadly than Blade's erection. The cry seemed loud enough to shake the flimsy hut down on the heads of the couple inside.

Sanaya cried out again, even louder. Her nails dug into Blade's back just below the shoulders and her legs flailed wildly in the air. He could feel her feet slamming against his hips and buttocks as he in turn slammed himself against her writhing body. Her arms locked about him tightly enough to make him gasp, and he felt an explosion of liquid warmth deep inside her and around him.

Somehow Blade came through Sanaya's climax and kept on thrusting. Now, though, he felt himself rising steadily toward his own peak, and he did not hold himself back. He swept upward, feeling like a bird borne upward by the wind. He swept upward toward his peak, and reached it.

Again a terrible cry filled the hut. Blade pressed downward, burying his face between Sanaya's breasts, clamping his hands tightly on her hips. He felt like sinking into her, dissolving away in the hot release of desire. He clung to her and she clung to him for a long moment. In that single moment there was almost tenderness.

Blade raised himself on his hands and kissed each of Sanaya's swollen nipples. Then he looked into her face, its frame of hair damp and straggly with sweat and matted with leaves from the floor. The queen's eyes were closed and her nostrils were wide as her starved lungs tried desperately to suck in air. But her lips were moving, repeating a pattern as she murmured the same words over and over again.

Blade listened. At first he heard only a meaningless noise. Then gradually the noise sorted itself into words he could understand.

Over and over again, Sanaya was murmuring, "King Blade, King Blade, King Blade, King Blade, King Blade."

King Blade! He had come to her out of desire, but also in the hope of finding out what games she might be playing. Desire was satisfied—Blade could not imagine feeling it again for hours, perhaps days. Now he had learned what he needed to know.

So he was "King Blade" to Sanaya, was he? So she wanted to see him beside her on the throne of Draad, and Embor and Neena cast down?

So what would she say and do when she found that he would not help her?

Chapter 20

It was well on into the afternoon when Blade left the hut. He and Sanaya drank beer from a jug and ate dried meat from a leather bag. Then somehow they found the strength to join again. By the time they were done, the queen was falling asleep.

Blade rose, put on his clothes, and peered through a crack in the wall out into the clearing. He could see the telltale movements of the watching guards among the trees. He could safely leave the queen to their care, and make his way back to the workshop.

Blade said nothing and kept his hands carefully in view until he was well out of sight of the clearing and the hut. He was mildly relieved to be able to get that far without a spear or an arrow in his back. The queen had no doubt given orders against harming him. But there was always somebody who didn't get the word, or who was too quick on the draw.

Once he was out of sight of the clearing, Blade settled down to his steady, mile-eating stride. His memory of the path guided him swiftly through the forest, where the mist now hung and coiled thicker than ever.

The clouds were as heavy in the evening as they had been in the morning, and the light went fast. It was almost totally dark by the time Blade reached the main path up to the workshop. By the time he saw the hearth glow from inside the walls, night had fallen on the forest and the mountains.

Three of the mountain hunters were sitting by the gate as Blade approached. They stood up and raised their spears as they saw him, then stepped aside as they recognized him. A moment later Blade heard footsteps behind the gate, and it was pulled open from inside. Blade entered, to meet Kulo.

The young man embraced Blade in his joy at his master's safe return, then shut the gate behind them. Blade could see that Kulo was excited about something more. He followed the young man into the workshop, and waited while Kulo took something long and wrapped in peza leaves from a bench.

"Look at it, Master Prince. I saw the drawings you made, and they started me thinking. I thought until I knew what we needed, and then I made it. Look at it, and see if my hands have made what we need."

Blade untied the peza leaves, let them fall to the floor, and examined what he held in his hands. It was a six-foot length of threebo. At one end was one of the natural partitions between the sections. Looking closely, Blade saw that a small hole had been drilled or punched in the partition.

Sticking out of the other end of the stalk was the wooden knob of something that looked like a plunger.

"Draw it out, Master Prince, and then push it in," said Kulo.

Blade hefted the odd weapon. It was heavier than it should have been.

120

"What did you put—?"

"Oh, Master Prince, I would not be so foolish as to use the new sleeping water. No, there is nothing in it but water from the spring."

So Kulo had indeed guessed what the workshop and its affairs were all about. Not surprising. If Kulo had the wit to work up an effective sprayer for the sleeping water from Blade's rough sketches, he had the wit to do a great many other things as well.

Blade pointed the sprayer away from them, drew the plunger out to its full length, then pushed it in with all his strength. There was no sound of leakage—Kulo had done his work well. Instead there was a sharp hiss, and a thin spray of water, almost mist-fine, shot out of the other end of the threebo. It lengthened as Blade drove in the plunger, until it reached out twenty feet or more.

Too late Blade saw what was about to happen. He swung the sprayer to one side, but not before the jetting mist of water fell on the red-hot coals of the forge. Steam exploded upward with a thunderous hiss and crackle, and live coals shot out of the hearth like meteors and fell to the floor. Kulo practically fell over his own feet, dashing to get a bucket of water to douse them. By the time he'd finished, the steam and smoke in the room were nearly as thick as the mist outside.

When Kulo finished cleaning up, Blade was waiting for him, hand outstretched. The young man hesitated, then took the hand, and Blade slapped him on the shoulder.

"Well done, Kulo. We don't know for certain how strong the stolofs are, of course. So we may need to make the sprayers bigger and stronger, to hold more water. Otherwise I think you've done most of the work. King Embor will hear of this, and I don't doubt that you will be hearing from him when he does."

A day spent rather badly was ending well, even triumphantly, and Blade felt surprisingly at peace with the world.

Blade did not allow himself to enjoy that feeling very long. There was far too much still to be done.

The method for distilling a stronger sleeping water was already worked out. Kulo's design would do for a sprayer. These made a good beginning, but that was all.

There weren't enough sprayers and water at the moment even for a good test, let alone a battle or a war against Trawn. Gallons of water and a dozen sprayers would be needed for the test alone. Dozens of barrels of the water and hundreds of sprayers would be needed for serious fighting, and so would hundreds of men trained in the tactics of using them. These tactics would be dangerous and they would require great speed and skill. Blade had no doubts about the courage of the warriors of Draad. But could they learn the speed and skill?

Blade realized that soon he would have more jobs than he could handle. He was already Director of Research and Development. Before long he would have to become Minister of War Production, and then Director of Training for His Majesty King Embor's Armed Forces! He had told J several times over that he was a field man, with little gift for administration. Yet here he was, up to his neck in just exactly that, and things were going to get much worse before they got any better!

For the time being, Blade decided that he would stick with the men and the equipment he had. In a few weeks he could produce everything that would be needed for a full-scale test, and then he could show off what he'd done.

There was also Queen Sanaya. Blade was sure he would be getting more invitations to come out into the forest and make love to her. If that was as far as matters went, well and good. Sooner or later, though, Sanaya would have more in mind than her own pleasures.

At least there was little chance of her finding out what he was doing here in the workshop. If Sanaya's guards wandered too close too often, the mountain hunters would know what to do about them, and do it without asking permission of Blade or anyone else. No, the secret was safe enough for the moment, even if Blade himself might not be.

So Blade went back to work with reasonable peace of mind.

He put in longer hours than ever over the next week. Again an invitation came from Queen Sanaya, and again Blade was led through the forests and over the hills to her hut. Again they met in what was almost more a battle than lovemaking, and again Blade was home in time for a night's sleep. This time Sanaya said nothing about "King Blade," or anything else revealing. Blade had no intention of asking too many leading questions, either.

A second week, a third, a fourth passed in the same way. The sleeping water was steadily accumulating, in large pots and small leather bottles. Kulo had made a dozen of the sprayers himself and was now teaching the other three assistants to make them. Soon there would be more than enough for any test.

Blade found himself still getting tired and still losing weight. It was not surprising. Six days of each week he worked eighteen hours a day. On the seventh day he tramped across the hills to couple with Queen Sanaya in her hut. Blade was as tough and indestructible as any human being could be, but he was still human.

The fifth week came, and went by without any invitations from Sanaya. Blade decided that the time was at hand for the test, and sent one of the assistants down the mountains to carry that message. He also sent an escort of six of the mountain hunters with the messenger. There were rumors of scouting parties and raiders from Trawn farther than ever before, with stolofs and even the rare riding meytans. It was unlikely the raiders would push this far, but Blade was taking no chances.

The day after the messenger left, Kulo came running in to announce that three warriors of the king's guard were approaching. Blade washed himself hastily, pulled on some respectable clothes, and went out to greet them.

"Blade," said the leader. "King Embor approaches. With him are the queen and Princess Neena, also various clan chiefs and their guards."

"I am greatly honored—" began Blade politely. The leader cut him off with a gesture.

"Hear us. They come to see what you have done with what you have been given, for the greatness of Draad.

123

They must be satisfied that you have done well, or it will go ill with you."

Blade nodded, but he did not like the leader's words or his tone. Something was badly wrong—he was under suspicion. It was hard to even tell *what* was wrong. He had given Queen Sanaya no reason that he knew to tell lies. Unless she had, this royal visit made no sense.

Damn! Blade did not like being pitchforked into dangerous situations where he didn't even know which way to look for the danger. There was only one thing to do: try to look in all directions at once.

Chapter 21

The royal party arrived shortly after breakfast the next morning. There were at least a hundred people in it, but Blade had eyes for only four: King Embor, Queen Sanaya, Princess Neena, and the High Kaireen.

Clean and well dressed, Blade advanced down the path toward Embor. Kulo walked behind him and the other three assistants followed Kulo. Blade carried a bottle of the sleeping water, and Kulo carried a sprayer.

King Embor halted the party as Blade approached. Then he motioned for the warriors on the flanks to close in around Blade and his assistants. Blade had the uncomfortable feeling that they were watching for him to make some suspicious move.

The king bore himself with even more dignity than usual, standing so straight that he seemed to tower even over Blade. Queen Sanaya was smiling, but the expression on Neena's face was unmistakable. Anger, suspicion, fear—and jealousy—all fought each other for control. Blade tried to meet her eyes, but she turned her face away from him, until her father noticed what she was doing and glared at her. Slowly Neena looked back toward Blade and stared at him defiantly.

Then the king spoke. "Prince Blade, you have had

much time to work upon what you promised to make for us. Have you done what you promised?"

The king's tone was almost completely expressionless, which was more of a surprise to Blade than outright hostility. He decided that whatever was going on here wasn't going to fit into *any* category.

"That is for you to judge, my Lord King," he replied. "I have worked hard and done my best. Kulo here has also worked well, and I pray you will see fit to reward him." Regardless of what happened to himself, Blade was determined to see that Kulo got credit for what he'd done. The young man deserved it.

"I have come to judge your work, Blade," said the king. The same neutral voice. "What you have done will be properly tested, and soon." He turned away from Blade and raised his voice to a commanding shout.

"Ho, guards. Forward, to make camp. Then begin the testing arena for Prince Blade."

What King Embor meant by "the testing arena" was soon obvious. A party of about forty warriors and servants marched a short distance downhill. Then they began cutting down every tree in a circle about fifty feet across. As the trees crashed down, they were hauled to the edge of the circle and piled up to form a high, thick wall around it.

This took most of the day. Before darkness fell, the men moved still farther downhill. They chopped down more trees and began building rough log enclosures.

The king explained. "Tomorrow the hunting parties will go out. They will catch wild animals of every kind they can find, and put them in those cages. When we have enough animals, you will go into the arena." He pointed at the large circular walled area. "Then the wild animals will be thrown into it, one by one, and we shall see—how well you have done what you promised."

Blade frowned. So he was going to have to play Roman gladiator, with his sprayer and sleeping water against whatever beasts the hunters might bring in. The water worked on insects and very small animals. That he already knew.

But a black stalker or one of the seventy-foot snakes would be another matter.

Certainly it would be as rigorous a test as anyone could wish. If he failed—well, failure in this case would carry its own swift and drastic penalties. That was probably exactly what King Embor had in mind, and perhaps Neena as well.

There was a problem, though.

"Do you think it is wise to show everyone what—what we may have done—so soon? The clan chiefs will be looking on, won't they?"

Embor nodded and looked around, to see if anyone was within earshot. Then he spoke quickly, in a low voice. "Blade, it is absolutely necessary that what you have done be shown to everyone, especially the clan chiefs. Believe me when I say that this is the only way."

For the first time since he'd arrived, Embor's voice had not been carefully neutral. The king was in deadly earnest about something exceedingly important. Blade still despaired of making any sense of what was going on, but decided to play along the way the king wanted it.

The mystery deepened for Blade during the days it took to catch and bring in all the test animals. Neena was obviously avoiding him. She would look at him or speak to him only when there were other people around. Then both her face and her voice would be cold and expressionless, and she would talk about nothing more personal than the weather or the progress of the hunting. Obviously she wouldn't have even said that much if King Embor hadn't been pushing her to keep up appearances.

There was also Queen Sanaya. She had no chance for a private word with Blade and apparently wasn't looking for any. But she spoke to him freely enough in public, politely and even graciously. She gave no sign that she had anything at all unusual on her mind. She seemed to be perpetually smiling, laughing, taking the king's arm. She seemed to be treating this unexpected stay in the Mountains of Hoga as a sort of picnic.

Blade found relief from wondering what plots were

126

waiting to spring out at him in watching the hunters bringing in the animals he would have to overcome. They made an impressive array, and the huts and enclosures were quickly filled. The camp was already a noisy place, with the crackle of campfires, the drums and flutes of King Embor's musicians, and the drunken singing of the warriors at night driving away the normal brooding quiet of the forests. Now the animals added to the noise, with a continuous chorus of hissings, screechings, growls, howls, twitterings, and other less describable sounds. The uproar must have been audible for miles. No one in this part of the forest could have any doubt that something unusual was going on.

That would include raiders from Trawn, if there were any around. Blade almost hoped there were. He would be happier if he knew how the sleeping water worked on actual live stolofs before risking a fullscale battle. The hunters of Draad couldn't very well go out and bring him back a batch of the creatures. But if the warriors of Trawn attacked and dumped some into his lap?

Meanwhile, he had various kinds of flightless birds. He had things like three-foot-long chipmunks, he had gray and black spotted deer with a single horn curving backward between the ears. He had a snake fourteen feet long with poison fangs as long as his fingers and alarmingly swift movements. He also had black stalkers.

The hunters brought in four of them, and they lost three men dead and two more crippled for life while doing so. That was something else Blade knew would be held against him if his inventions were unsuccessful.

The black stalkers had the heavy-bodied build of home dimension wildcats. But they were the size of small tigers—three hundred pounds or more. They were swift and sure in their movements, and their mouths were a foot wide and set with an array of teeth that would have done credit to a shark. Their large yellow eyes followed Blade grimly and unwaveringly as he walked around the stout huts where they were confined. He looked back at them just as carefully. All the other animals would just be warming-up exercises, even the snake. The black stalkers would be the real test.

He wished he could be as sure who were his real *human* enemies.

Chapter 22

The next morning the blare of trumpets and the squalling of black stalkers sounded well before dawn. Blade was already awake when Kulo came in to help him dress and equip himself.

Blade pulled on a hunter's tunic and trousers of heavy green leather, reinforced over the chest, belly, and groin. He donned a warrior's leather helmet and thick-soled boots. He belted on a short sword and dagger. Then he picked up a sprayer and hung three bottles of sleeping water on his belt.

Blade started down the hill toward the arena. Behind him marched Kulo, dressed like Blade but looking thoroughly uncomfortable in the unfamiliar leather garments and boots. He had volunteered to enter the arena with Blade; therefore he wore the same clothes. Behind Kulo marched the other three assistants, carrying everything Blade thought might possibly be needed at the arena.

The sky overhead had turned from gray to blue by the time Blade reached the arena. It was going to be a sunny day, a rare event in the mountain forests. Blade felt his mood lighten as he saw the sunlight flash gold through the branches of the trees that towered up on either side of the path.

The log walls of the arena rose more than ten feet high. Around the outside warriors wearing the badges of Embor, Sanaya, and half a dozen different clans stood on guard.

On top of the log walls of the arena the king, the queen, Neena, the High Kaireen, and the rest of the notables were already in place. Some sat on benches, others squatted Indian-fashion on the bare, peeled logs. The wall of the arena rose half again as high as a black stalker could jump. The notables would be in no danger, whatever happened to Blade and Kulo.

Blade led his assistants up the ladder on the outside of the wall. Neena met his gaze but her face was chill. King Embor smiled in greeting, but thinly. Blade noticed that both of them wore fighting gear. Neena had two spears propped against her bench and the king had a bow slung across his back and a sword at his belt.

Queen Sanaya, on the other hand, once more seemed as cheerful as if she were on a picnic. She wore a red gown and white leather boots, with a dark brown fur robe thrown over her shoulders. A tiara of emeralds sparkled in her hair as she looked around her, laughing and chattering to everyone within earshot. She had the look of someone for whom the day could hold no unpleasant surprises.

Another ladder led down to the floor of the arena. The three assistants sat down on the logs and began unpacking the gear while Blade and Kulo climbed down the wobbling, hastily made ladder. Blade hoped he wouldn't have to climb that ladder in any sort of a hurry.

Blade checked his weapons, climbed up onto a stump, and looked out across the arena. On the opposite side of the circle, fifty feet away, was a gate of heavy logs for the test animals.

Blade motioned Kulo to stand well behind him. Then he looked up at the royal party. King Embor nodded and raised his hand. On top of the wall and from outside it horns and drums sounded to signal the beginning of the test. With grindings and creakings of wood, the gate started to swing open. Blade gripped his sprayer, wondering what would come through. King Embor had politely refused to let him know the order in which the animals would be released.

Then a faint *clurk—clurk—clurk* sounded from across the arena, followed by the sound of clumsily flapping wings. Blade laughed. The first test specimen was a

129

mugos—a slow-witted, ground-dwelling bird about the size and shape of a Home Dimension turkey.

Blade strode forward. As the bird spotted him it *clurked* in alarm and darted back toward the gate. Finding the gate closed, it jumped on top of a stump and flapped its wings frantically. By that time Blade was within easy range. He raised the sprayer, aimed it at the bird's head, and rammed in the plunger.

The six feet of threebo jumped as Blade fired, and the fine spray missed the bird completely. He shifted one hand to get a better grip, then aimed and fired again. This time he hit his target. The bird blinked in surprise and bewilderment as the sleeping water doused it. It opened its beak to complain. Then it tottered, its eyes closed, and it fell forward off the stump with a faint plop.

Blade looked around the walls of the arena. Everyone was on his feet. Several of the clan chiefs were pointing at the fallen bird, openmouthed with unconcealed astonishment. Blade saw King Embor's thin smile changing into a grin. Watching the clan chiefs gaping like schoolboys must be a treat for him! Well, there were going to be a good many more surprises before this day was over.

The guards outside the gate came in, took the bird away, and led in one of the giant chipmunks. This animal was much more intelligent and quicker on its feet than the bird. It darted around and around the arena, ducking in and out behind the stumps, sometimes jumping up on top of one to chatter mockingly at Blade. Blade sprayed several doses of sleeping water into thin air, trying to hit it.

Now Blade waved Kulo forward. With the young man well out ahead of him, he managed to trap the animal against one wall. It tried to leap over a stump, but a shot from Kulo's sprayer caught it in midair. It landed sprawling, lurched to its feet, took two steps, then fell flat on its face and lay still.

This brought all the clan chiefs to their feet again. Several shouted out loud. They hadn't been told what they might expect to see from Prince Blade. Probably none of them even now understood exactly what was going on. But they could see skill and speed at work, and most of them could appreciate that. Blade threw a glance at Neena. She was obviously struggling not to smile. Sanaya was laughing out loud.

There was a pause, while servants walked precariously along the wall, handing mugs of beer and plates of sausage and roast meat to the spectators. Then the guards drove one of the single-horned deer in through the gate.

Blade knew that this animal would be a somewhat more drastic test than the ones before. It was many times larger, and would therefore need a much larger dose of sleeping water. In the confined arena it could not run as freely and swiftly as it could in the forest, but it would still be a difficult target. It was also capable of defending itself. That made Blade feel a good deal more comfortable about going after it. He didn't much like shooting things at birds and animals who could do nothing in return except run.

He stepped toward the deer. It lowered its head until the point of the horn was low enough to hook upward. Large black eyes rimmed with white stared at Blade. The stag made a low bubbling sound in its throat. Then it charged straight at Blade.

Blade's first shot of sleeping water went right over the stag's head and struck halfway down its back. A patch of hair turned dark and damp. That was all. Before Kulo could fire, the stag was on them.

Blade darted to one side, Kulo to the other. The stag made an incredibly sharp turn and followed Kulo. Worried about not appearing a coward before his king and so many warriors, the young man was a little slow off the mark. The stag caught up with him and the horn hooked upward. Kulo rose into the air, sailed over a stump, and kept on running. A long, neat slash gaped in the seat of his leather trousers. A surgeon with a scalpel couldn't have done a better job. On the wall above, the gasps of surprise turned into roars of laughter.

Blade vaulted high over two stumps in a single bound and came down beside the stag as it turned to pursue Kulo. He swung the heavy sprayer like a quarterstaff, smacking the stag across the back of the neck. As it turned to face him, Blade aimed and fired a quick shot that hit squarely on its long black-furred nose.

The stag reared back on its hind legs in surprise, then dropped back onto all fours. Its nostrils flared. Its eyes remained open, but they seemed curiously unfocused. Then it tried to take a step toward Blade, nearly fell to its knees, and stood wobbling and motionless. Blade walked up to it and scratched it between its floppy ears, then ran a hand along its back. The stag trembled but did not move or even look at Blade.

Blade raised a hand in salute to the royal party. "With your permission—shall it go free? It has done its part, and bravely."

King Embor nodded. "By all means, let it go. It is no enemy of ours—although Kulo might have something to say on that." Everyone joined in the laugh, including Kulo.

Letting the stag go was easier said than done. Blade went around behind it and slapped it on the rump. It shivered but didn't move. He went back to the head and tried to push it around toward the gate. Nothing happened. Kulo pushed with both hands on its rump while Blade pulled with both hands on its horn. Still no results. By this time all the spectators were half-hysterical with laughter, and some of them looked ready to fall off the wall.

"Well, we can't say we didn't stop the stag," Blade muttered to himself. "In fact we did the job too bloody well!" Sweat was streaming down both his face and Kulo's, and he alternately felt like cursing and laughing.

Eventually they had to call six guards into the arena. The men picked up the stag as if it had been a statue— one at the head, one at the rump, four in the middle. Then they staggered out of the arena with it, and Blade never did find out what happened to the stag after that. He hoped it didn't end up as venison for the guards' next dinner.

At this point Blade noticed that Queen Sanaya was no longer in sight. He was about to call a question up to

King Embor when the king shouted down, "Hold for a time, Blade. The queen feels faint. She has gone to lie in the shade for a time, with her personal Kaireen to attend her."

There was something in that tale that didn't ring quite true in Blade's ears. It was also obvious that King Embor wouldn't have told it if there wasn't some good reason for having it believed by everyone within earshot.

"Very well," he shouted back. "We shall wait until our lady queen returns. Let my other three assistants come down."

The three assistants climbed slowly down the rickety ladder. Blade and Kulo drank water, nibbled cheese and sausage, checked and refilled their sprayers, then sat down to wait. Blade took out a sharpening stone and set out to improve the edge on his sword.

The sky was completely clear by now, and the sun was getting positively hot. In the arena the log walls cut off much of the breeze. Blade sat on a stump, listening to the drone of insects and the steady *scrrrp-scrrrp* of stone on steel, smelling the odors of mold and resin, thinking of nothing in particular.

An hour passed. Blade began to wonder if Queen Sanaya was really ill, and if so, what was wrong with her. He also couldn't help wondering if this was a natural illness, or had one of her enemies taken a hand in the matter?

More immediately important to him, what animal would come through the gate first when the testing started again? It might be another stag. It might be the snake. Or it might be one of the black stalkers. It had to be one of those three. The stag and the snake held no real danger. The black stalkers, on the other hand—

Someone shouted from the ground outside the arena. It was a high-pitched shout, almost a scream, filled with surprise and fear. Several people on the wall turned to stare down, then suddenly sprang to their feet with more shouts. Blade saw Neena snatch up one of her spears, turn, and raise it, ready to throw.

133

Then for the first time someone shouted out in words. "The black stalkers are loose!"

A moment later the gate was hurled aside. It crashed to the ground, and two black stalkers came leaping in through the opening. Their mouths were wide and foam-flecked, and their eyes red and ghastly.

As they saw Blade and Kulo, they let out their terrible hunting screams. Neena's scream echoed theirs. Then the two animals sprang toward Blade and Kulo.

Chapter 23

Neena's spear whistled down from the wall. Normally she had a deadly eye and arm, but these creatures were moving too fast even for her. The spear sank into a stump. The second stalker leaped clear over it, knocking it to the ground, and charged on.

The two creatures seemed to come at Blade like shots from a gun. One moment they were leaping in through the gate. The next moment they were leaping at his throat.

As fast as they were, Blade was faster. In the hope of confusing them he leaped forward, passing between them. A heavy black-furred hind leg brushed against his shoulder. The stalker felt the touch and tried to lash out at Blade's head while still in midair. Blade ducked in time, and the claws missed his cheek by an impossibly thin margin. The stalker landed off balance and could not turn and spring at once. As the creature turned, so did Blade. He drove the end of his sprayer into its face, then slapped the plunger with his other hand.

The spray came out with a pitiful little wheeze. For all the effect it had on the black stalker, it might as well have been milk. The creature gave a tremendous scream and leaped again. Blade threw himself to his knees as the stalker rose into the air, and it sailed over his head to land on a stump behind him.

This time he had a few seconds before the creature leaped again. He risked taking his eyes off it to look around. The three assistants were all swarming up the ladder as fast as they could. As the last one scrambled to safety, the ladder gave a sharp crack and split in the middle. The two halves thudded down onto the floor of the arena.

Kulo was standing his ground, torn trousers and all. Blade wouldn't have blamed the young man if he'd led the flight of the assistants. Once more Kulo seemed determined to show a warrior's courage. Blade wasn't sure whether this was showing good sense or not, but it was too late now to do anything else.

A hideous scream rose from outside the wall, and Neena threw her other spear. Blade saw her leap up and down, shaking her fists at her own poor marksmanship. The screams went on, mixed with the furious growls of a black stalker.

"Kulo!" he roared. "Don't try to spray them! They're drugged or mad!" For all their ferocity, Blade had never heard of black stalkers attacking in this frenzied way. There was something unnatural and horrible about it, as well as deadly dangerous. Did the madness of the stalkers have anything to do with Queen Sanaya's "illness"?

Then Blade forgot about Queen Sanaya, Neena, Kulo, the poor wretch dying in agony outside the wall, everything else except the three hundred pounds of black-furred death hurling itself at him.

He held the sprayer crosswise at arm's length in front of him. It met the black stalker in midleap, slamming hard into the creature's broad chest. The tough, resin-bound wood held, but the shock was enough to knock Blade backward off his feet. He landed on his back with the creature on top of him.

Both wits and muscles worked even faster than before. Blade slammed the threebo up and forward, into the stalker's gaping, drooling jaws as they opened above him. The jaws clamped shut like a hydraulic press. That was too much even for the threebo, and the sprayer snapped. All the sleeping water gushed out into the black stalker's mouth. As Blade struggled to draw his sword and thrust upward into the creature's throat, it gave one tremendous gasp and went limp. A moment later its eyes closed and Blade was able to roll out from under the dead body.

As he staggered to his feet he heard Kulo give a horrible scream. Blade whirled to see the young man go down under the leap of the other black stalker. Kulo screamed a second time as the claws tore at his shoulders and chest. By some miracle he was able to clamp his hands around the creature's throat, pushing its head back far enough to keep the teeth away from his own throat. The teeth snapped together inches from his nose, and the stalker growled and snarled in raw fury.

Blade drew his sword, sprang onto a stump, then down from the stump onto the stalker's back. His two hundred pounds drove his heavy boots down on the creature's back. It sprawled flat on Kulo, momentarily stunned. Then Blade slashed downward. The sharpened edge of his sword sliced through fur, skin, and flesh, biting into the spine. The black stalker howled in agony, gave one convulsive twist that threw Blade sprawling, and died.

Blade leaped to his feet and dragged the dead stalker off Kulo. Mercifully, the young man was unconscious. His shoulders and chest were a mass of shredded, blood-soaked leather and torn flesh. But he still breathed, and there was no blood bubbling out of his mouth to indicate internal injuries. Luck and the care of the Kaireens might pull him through.

As Blade stood up from his examination of Kulo, he heard someone call his name. As he turned around, Neena dashed toward him, tears streaking the dust on her face. She threw herself into his arms, her lips pressing warmly and hungrily against his. Her hands stroked his hair, and after a moment his arms seemed to rise of their own accord and tighten around her.

Then King Embor stepped up to them and coughed softly to get their attention. Slowly they stepped apart and faced him, still holding hands.

Blade's heart still pounded, his breath still came in

gasps, and sweat still poured down off him in streams. His mind was working clearly again.

"Neena, my Lord King. Tell me—*what the bloody hell is going on around here?*"

Neena spoke before King Embor could even open his mouth. "Blade, I have done you a terrible wrong. I have been jealous of you and Queen Sanaya, and yet I see now that—"

King Embor coughed again. "Blade, it were better that I spoke of this. If my foolish, jealous, loving daughter who is your wife tries to speak of it, the sun will be down before you understand what happened. I think you do not wish to wait that long. Is that not so?"

Blade nodded. "Indeed it is. I gather that Queen Sanaya has had something to do with all this?"

"You are correct. Some weeks ago, mountain hunters found one of the queen's personal guards where he should not have been. By custom they would have killed him on the spot. But they thought it wiser to send him down into the valley and on to me.

"He was brought to me, and when he would not explain what he had done, he was tortured. Then he told a story of how you raped Queen Sanaya and held a long bout of love with her in a hut in the forest."

Blade nodded. "She did—let us say, she did bring me to her bed in such a place. She threatened to tell just that story if I refused her."

King Embor laughed bitterly. "That is what I thought, and what Neena should have realized." The princess nodded silently and squeezed Blade's hand more tightly. "Had Sanaya herself come to me with such a story, I would have laughed in her face. I did not know all of her qualities when I took her to wife, but I am not so old that I cannot see what goes on around me and learn from it. I know how much to believe of what she tells me."

"Nothing," put in Neena.

Embor nodded. "But the guard's tale was another matter. It seemed to me that he just might be telling the truth."

"I was sure he was," said Neena, with a catch in her voice. "Yet—"

137

Once more King Embor held up a hand for silence. "So perhaps you had indeed done me and Neena a considerable wrong. At the same time you were working hard for Draad, and your work might give us some hope of victory over Trawn. I could not set that hope aside, even for so great an offense. Yet if the secret of your crime were known, the jealousy of the clan chiefs would mean your death, and sooner rather than later.

"So Neena and I did what seemed the wisest thing. We told no one of what we thought you had done, except some of my oldest and most trusted guards. We also gave the order that your work was to be tested at once.

"If you had worked well, you would be too valuable to punish, whether or not you were guilty. Then the secret would die with us. If you had not done what you promised, it would make no difference to our people whether you lived or died. Then we would have risen to denounce you before all the chiefs of Draad, and your death would have followed swiftly."

Blade frowned. His escape had been even narrower than he'd suspected. "And now—?"

"Now you have shown us all the power of the new sleeping water. I have listened to the chiefs talking. Most of them have already realized what your invention could do to stolofs. Also, you have shown enormous skill and courage before them all." Embor laughed. "I think they would all fight to keep anything from happening to you, regardless of what you'd done."

Blade nodded. It seemed clear enough, so far. "What of the black stalkers, and all they did?" He pointed to where Kulo lay on the ground, still unconscious. The High Kaireen himself and two assistants were at work on him. They'd already cut away the leather tunic and were at work cleaning the wounds.

"We are not certain, now," said Neena. Her face was still very pale. "But somehow Sanaya learned—here, to-day—that we knew of her game. It was doubtless a shock to her, so perhaps she was really ill. In any case she was certainly in a panic."

At this point the High Kaireen joined them and took

138

up the tale. "The Kaireen she called to attend her was most foully in her pay. She told him to use certain drugs he had with him to drive the black stalkers into a mad frenzy. Then certain of her guards were to release them. This was done, and the rest you have seen." He faced the king, his deeply lined face grim. "Lord, have I your permission to take upon myself the punishment of the Kaireen who did this thing? He has dishonored and shamed all of us, and I assure you that he will trouble Draad no more."

"I see no reason why you should not do this," said the king. "But perhaps Prince Blade would care to speak. He was put in the greatest danger and a comrade of his lies desperately wounded."

"The Kaireens certainly have every right to punish their own traitors," said Blade. "What happened to the other stalkers?"

"Both are dead," said Embor. "But so are four of my guards. Six more will bear scars to the end of their lives."

"And Queen Sanaya?"

"She has fled into the forest," said Neena. "It hardly seems worth the trouble to hunt her down. She has no skill or swiftness in the woods, and death will overtake her without our help."

Blade frowned. "I am not so sure of that. Terror can give skill and speed to anyone. Even if she does die, she may live long enough to reach those who ought not to hear of what she has seen today."

He looked at King Embor, the High Kaireen, and Neena. All three of them nodded.

Chapter 24

Queen Sanaya ran through the forest. She didn't know where she was running, and didn't care. She knew that she ran from King Embor, and also from Neena and from Blade. She ran from death, because those three people

139

knew everything she had tried to do. They would kill her if she didn't run. She didn't care how little she knew about the forests or the Mountains of Hoga and how to live in them. She didn't know or care how long her strength would last. She only knew that it would last somehow until she was far away from the arena, even if she dropped down dead the moment after that.

She almost hoped she would. It would be a quicker death than dying of hunger or snake bite. That death in turn would be quicker than what Embor and Blade would give her if they caught her. And as for Princess Neena— Sanaya sobbed aloud in fear at the thought of the princess going to work on her. A lingering remnant of sanity told her she should not waste her breath weeping. She ran on in silence.

She ran on until she had to slow down. Now she moved at a painful trot, then a walk, then a lurching stagger. She gasped for breath at each step. At each gasp it felt as if molten metal was rising up in her throat. Her head throbbed until it seemed that it would split open and let her brains ooze out. Her eyes watered, then streamed; she felt the salt of tears on her lips, mixing with blood. Somewhere at some moment she had bitten deep into her lower lip.

She felt cold, damp earth and slickly wet leaves against her feet and looked down. Her boots were soft leather, designed for show, not for hard walking and still less for running in the forest. Both boots were ripped and worn through. The skin of her feet already showed darkening bruises made by stones and roots and thin red lines left by thorns.

She was afraid that if she stopped she would never start up again. She did not know how far she had come from the arena and her enemies. She only knew in her pounding heart and fear-ridden mind that she hadn't come far enough. The knowledge gave her the strength to stumble onward.

Some impossibly long time later, a jutting branch caught one boot and jerked it right off. Sanaya staggered and fell painfully forward on her hands and knees. She slumped down on her face and lay gasping for breath, as mindless as a wounded animal.

After a while strength returned to the muscles she needed for sitting up and stripping off the other boot. She noticed also that her fur cloak was gone, fallen from her shoulders somewhere now miles behind her. Below her knees her skirt was shredded by thorns and branches and dark with grass stains, mud, and dampness.

If she was strong enough to see clearly, she must be strong enough to move on again. She reached for a bush and held onto its branches, using them to pull herself to her feet. She swayed and staggered, but did not fall again. Her hands were dotted with oozing red punctures, from thorns she hadn't even felt.

The sunlight no longer sparkled down golden from high above. It was turning red and slanting in from the west. The day was dying; in another couple of hours it would be dead. But the day would live again, the next time the sun rose. If Blade or Neena caught her, she would die, and for her death would be final. *She would go on.*

She did, although a child just learning to walk could have gone as fast. Before long the skirt of her gown grew so heavy and wet that she stopped again to rip it off up to the knees.

The breeze now blew chill against her bare legs and bruised and swollen feet.

Before long the insects came to her. They whined in her ears, they made a cloud in front of her eyes, they bit furiously at every bit of exposed skin. Some of the bites left red and yellow blotches, others drew blood which drew more insects. She began to wonder if the dizziness and the blurred vision were still just fatigue. Or were poison and the loss of blood from insect bites beginning to take their toll? She did not know, she would never find out, and she could not afford to care.

How much longer Sanaya stumbled on through the gathering twilight, she never knew. When she finally felt her strength beginning to leave her for good, it was nearly dark. When she looked down at her feet, she now saw blood oozing up between the toes, and bloody footprints on the ground behind her. The insects swarmed more thickly. She groaned, and kept moving.

Suddenly the ground was dropping away in front of her. She staggered, and tried to throw herself backward. Legs where every joint and muscle flamed with a separate agony would not respond. She felt herself lurching forward, flailed wildly at the air, screamed, and fell.

She did not plunge down into a bottomless depth and smash herself to pieces. Instead she fell only a few feet, hit a steep slope overgrown with thorn bushes, and rolled. The thorns clawed and stabbed at her as she rolled.

Then she reached the bottom of the slope. Her head grazed a massive tree root, and pain even fiercer and sharper than before exploded behind her eyes. For a moment she saw nothing but darkness. For another moment she had the horrible feeling that she'd gone blind.

Through that darkness stabbed a man's loud, harsh voice. Then came the sound of footsteps, and a chittering sound Sanaya had never heard herself but heard described far too often. Blindly she tried to roll away from the approaching stolof. She did not worry about how it had come here. She only knew that she had to get away from it and from the man who must be its master.

A new pain burned as a whip slashed down across her bare legs, wrapping itself around them. She was dragged to a stop, and somehow the pain seemed to clear her vision. She twisted her head to look at the man standing over her.

He was tall and burly, with the unmistakable mark of a warrior noble of Trawn in the way he carried himself. He wore a tunic reinforced with copper bands, and across his broad back was slung a long curved two-handed sword. A long, ugly red scar ran down the right side of his face, from forehead to chin and just missing the eye. The eyes that glared down out of that face glittered with both an animal's mindless cruelty and a wise man's ability to think and scheme.

Panic roared and howled in Sanaya's mind again, drowning out everything else she could feel. She clawed at the ground, drooled, tried to jerk herself to her feet. The man let her rise to her knees. Then his fist smashed down like a thunderbolt, taking her on the side of the jaw. Sanaya sprawled backward on the ground, and this time the darkness did not go away for a long time.

When Sanaya did awake, she found herself lying on a dirt floor, looking up at a dirt ceiling and dirt walls. She was bound hand and foot with the skin-tearing cords of Trawn, and she was completely naked.

Pains itched, burned, and throbbed in every part of her body. She felt as though she had been torn into little pieces and then crudely and hastily put back together.

Gradually the pains stopped overpowering her awareness of everything else. She realized that she was in a tunnel or cave running deep into the side of a hill. By moving her head only a little she could see the mouth of the cave, a rough circle faintly defined by the distant glow of a campfire off in the forest. She could see the silhouettes of men moving back and forth across the mouth of the cave. Outbursts of chittering and a faintly sour, acrid odor told her of stolofs nearby.

She was in the hands of scouts or raiders from Trawn, who had crossed the Mountains of Hoga. They had stolofs, they had the strength and self-confidence to make camp in the forests and light fires. It would not be easy to escape from them, even if she regained her strength quickly.

Panic nearly swamped her again. She was in the hands of warriors of Trawn, with all their viciousness and cruelty. She was in the hands of perhaps the only people in all of Gleor who would kill her more painfully than Neena might. There was nothing she could do about it. THERE WAS NOTHING SHE COULD DO ABOUT IT!

"Yes, there is something you can do about it," said a voice from behind her. She gasped, realizing that she must have spoken her thoughts aloud.

The scar-faced nobleman sat cross-legged on the floor of the cave, staring at her. He wore only a short kilt and boots, and carried only a short sword. He held one of the long five-stranded whips of Trawn across his tanned knees. Involuntarily Sanaya's eyes focused on those knees and the man's muscular legs. Then she caught herself and quickly shifted her gaze. The man smiled, and Sanaya shivered as she realized that her little slip had not escaped his notice.

"Would you like to know what can be done about it?" he asked, his smile broadening. It was by no means a friendly or reassuring smile. It was more of an unpleasantly triumphant gloating over a prize.

Sanaya hadn't expected anything else from a warrior of Trawn. Her lips were trembling so badly that she could not speak in reply, but only nodded.

"You can start by telling me who you are," the warrior said. "You are clearly a woman of high rank in Draad. Yet you are in a most strange place and in an even stranger condition for one such. Who are you, and how did you come to be here?"

Now Sanaya could not even move a muscle, let alone speak coherent words. Behind the panic flickered one faint trace of rational thought. Nothing this man could do to her for keeping silent would be as horrible as he would do if she lied, or admitted who she was.

The warrior grunted and approached her until he could reach down and put a hand under her chin. He lifted it gently until her eyes met his. Then suddenly he tightened his grip so hard that his long dirty nails stabbed through Sanaya's skin into her flesh. She gasped at the sudden pain. Then the warrior drew back his other hand and brought it across Sanaya's face as hard as he could. She gasped again. If her head hadn't been held still, she would have sprawled backward.

The warrior spent a good deal of time working Sanaya over with slaps, punches, kicks, and pinches on any and every part of her body he could reach. She quickly lost track of the individual blows. They all blended together into one long torment that seemed as though it would go on forever.

Much to Sanaya's surprise, it did not. Eventually the warrior stopped and stepped back, leaving her lying on

144

the ground. Gradually her mind cleared until she could recognize all her different sensations.

She could not have spoken now if she'd wanted to—her lips were a swollen, ragged, bloody mess. More blood trickled from her aching nose and from where several teeth had been knocked out. Her eyes were swollen and watering so that everything around her seemed to be swimming through a thick bloodshot fog. Her nipples and thighs throbbed and burned where they'd been pinched, her fingers and toes ached where they'd been twisted, and large patches of skin felt as though they'd been burned. She wouldn't have dared to touch most of her own body, even if her hands had been free.

Yet somehow she did not feel as totally wretched as she'd expected. Other sensations were lurking behind the pain and exhaustion, like the hunters of the mountain clans lurking in the forest. She could not easily put a name to these other feelings. She could make a comparison that somehow made them comprehensible. She felt as she did with a lover, as his hands moved over her skin and cupped her breasts, and his lips pressed warmly against hers. She could almost imagine that Blade was here now, arousing her, and she closed her eyes to see if that would make the image more vivid.

Before she could find out, the warrior cursed. Then he grabbed her by the hair and jerked her to her feet. She opened her eyes to see that he was dragging her toward a tall, heavy wooden stake driven into the floor of the cave.

The warrior tied her ankles tightly to the stake. Then he pulled both her arms high up over her head, and tied her wrists to the stake. From chin to knees she was pressed hard against the rough wood, unable to writhe or twist, barely able to breathe. She had to stand nearly on tiptoe to keep her arms and wrists from being pulled out of joint, and wondered how long she would be able to hold that position. Her weary legs and ankles already throbbed and ached enough.

The warrior picked up the whip and stepped to one side, where she could easily see him. Then he swung the whip several times at the empty air, flicking his wrist each time so that the tips of all five strands cracked like snapping branches. Sanaya could not take her eyes off the whip and the arm that was wielding it, which was no doubt exactly what the warrior intended. It was the vicious torture whip of Trawn, and the arm wielding it was thick and knotted with muscle. Once the warrior started in on her, he could doubtless go on for hours. If Sanaya's stomach hadn't been totally empty, she would have vomited at the prospect. At the same time she felt a faint curiosity to feel the whip on her flesh. The strange feeling that a lover was at work arousing her was still there, and the combination would be—well, oddly interesting, as well as horribly painful.

"*Now* are you interested in telling me who you are?" said the warrior. He seemed indifferent to whether she answered or not. She suspected he would be quite happy to have an excuse to go to work with his whip.

A moment later she knew she was right. A broad grin spread across the warrior's face, and his arm stretched out. The grin broadened as the whip lashed back, then forward. The whip came down across the small of Sanaya's back, and she never saw what happened to the grin after that. The world around her vanished as pain exploded up from where the whip fell, into her brain and out to every part of her body. She screamed. Before she finished screaming the whip came down again, this time across the backs of her thighs.

Five, ten, fifteen times the whip struck, each time a little bit harder, each time in a more sensitive spot. The pain was passing onward into something which Sanaya's reeling mind could find no words to describe. Each time she told herself that she could stand no more, that the next stroke would kill her. Yet the next stroke always came, and she always found herself alive.

She might have died or fainted eventually, except that before long she was feeling more than pain. The feeling that a lover was at work on her came again, more vividly. Now it was no longer just tongue and lips and hands that she could imagine. Now it was a swollen, rigid, thrusting maleness driving deep into her, forcing her desire to a

146

higher and higher pitch, making her more and more of an animal. The pain of the whip remained. But now each time it fell there was more than pain. There seemed to be a long thrust by her phantom lover, driving deep into her, withdrawing slowly, tantalizing her, torturing her in a way that was almost more agonizing than the whip.

Her lips began to move, and incoherent sounds that were not at all human came from her throat. She drove her groin and breasts against the stake, feeling more pain as tender flesh met hard rough wood. Yet she also felt as if her lover's own passion and his own vigor were steadily increasing.

All her pain and all her pleasure combined to fog both her eyes and her mind until she could no longer see anything or make any sense of what she felt. She was hardly aware of coming to her climax, writhing and shrieking and howling so loudly that all the men on guard outside leaped up and grabbed weapons, thinking that the camp was being attacked. She was even less aware of the warrior cutting her down, stripping off his kilt, and taking her furiously as she writhed on the floor. She fainted completely before she could see the warrior's face above her. That face was twisted by the release of a terrible passion, but also by a cold and calculating satisfaction.

Lord Desgo had reason to be satisfied. He was still not sure entirely who or what he had in his hands. But certainly she had a high place in Draad, high enough to know much of what he needed to know before his army struck. Just as certainly, she would not hold back any of it. Not now, for he had found the love of pain that lurked in her soul. As long as he could satisfy that love she would be his slave in all but name.

Lord Desgo was not a fool, and he admitted that luck had been with him in bringing to him a woman with that kind of soul. Not all women had it. Princess Neena, for example, had no great love of pain—only a great hatred for him. Dealing with her as she deserved would be no pleasure for her—only for him. He would have that pleasure, though. He promised himself that. King Furzun himself would not stand between him and Neena's death now.

Although he had released his passion only a few minutes before, Lord Desgo found it rising again at the thought of Neena's long lingering death at his hands. So he put Neena out of his mind and returned to the woman beside him, who now received him with furious pleasure.

Chapter 25

For Blade and Neena, the days after the testing and Sanaya's disappearance seemed to fly past, one after another, in rapid succession, like migrating birds. There were enough things to do each day to fill many more than twenty-four hours. Yet somehow they found a little time to spend together.

"Your work and my jealousy and anger kept us apart for too long," Neena said. "That was an evil time, but now it is over."

There were a dozen things for Blade to do himself and as many more things to supervise. There were sprayers and sleeping water to make in vast quantities, there were hundreds of warriors to train in using the sprayers, there were new battle tactics to devise and teach for the whole army of Draad. There were enough things to keep three Richard Blades busy, an idea that Neena found rather amusing.

"I suppose that if there were three of you, I could keep one with me and let the other two work all the time." She bit him gently on the ear. "But they'd have to be absolutely *identical*. I would not take any imitations." Her lips moved down his body and conversation came to an end for quite a while.

Fortunately all of Blade's work showed results. Kulo had taught the other three assistants well. They in turn taught dozens of craftsmen how to make the sprayers. Soon there were more of them than the workshop could hold, and Blade had a shed built to store the overflow.

Beside the shed for the sprayers stood another shed where bottles and jars of the sleeping water soon rose to the ceiling. A dozen stills now worked around the clock. Before long there would be enough sleeping water to slay all the stolofs in Trawn five times over.

Most of the water would go into the sprayers, but some was poured into small clay pots. In the coming battles these pots would be thrown at stolofs or their masters. They were not as accurate as the sprayers, but they could be thrown from beyond the range of a stolof's ribbon. Every warrior trained as a stolof killer would have both a sack of pots on his back and a sprayer in his hands.

There would be a great many such warriors—or at least Blade intended that there would be, given enough time. He did not know if there would be enough time, so he pushed the training as if the armies of Trawn were already marching through the passes of the Mountains of Hoga.

For training, he used a method he had used before. He taught ten selected warriors and hunters (including King Embor and Neena) how to use the sprayers and pots, then had each of them teach ten more, and so on. Within a few days more than a thousand fighting men of Draad at least knew one end of a sprayer from the other. Within a few more days most of them could hit what they fired at more than half the time.

That was a good start. Blade had no intention of training all the fighting men of Draad to be stolof killers, in any case. There would be only so many stolofs to kill. The rest of Trawn's army would be human warriors, and swords, spears, arrows, axes, and clubs would do for them.

Blade was not entirely free of worries, however. Reports continued to come in from the clansmen, telling of more and more raiders from Trawn in the mountains. A few parties were attacked and wiped out, but no prisoners were taken, and even these victories were few.

The coming of such a mass of raiders—or scouts—from Trawn made Blade wonder. It was hard to see what else could be following them except an invading army.

"Would you like to have more warriors camping up here to guard the workshop?" King Embor asked Blade.

Blade shook his head. "The camp of the stolof killers is only two miles down the hill. That is close enough so that they can reach the workshop quickly, without staying around here."

Embor nodded in understanding. "The secret, again?"

"Yes," said Blade. "Of course, many now know what our weapon is, and how to use it. But few know how it is made. I would rather things stayed that way until we have met and destroyed the army of Trawn. There is a risk in leaving the workshop weakly guarded, but it is one I think we can afford better than having the secret leak out."

Embor did send a good many warriors to watch each of the passes through the Mountains of Hoga. That way no large force from Trawn could get through and devastate the lands of Draad without being detected at once and brought to battle soon afterward. The king also set up a line of warriors stretching from the workshop down to the camp of the stolof killers. Each warrior stood within shouting distance of the next. Word of any danger could fly along the line to the camp much faster than a man could run. King Embor was an excellent strategist and leader; Blade was not worried about leaving that part of the campaign in his hands for now.

He still worried at times over what might have happened to Queen Sanaya. Her fur cloak had been found, and one shredded, bloodstained boot. Did that mean she had been attacked and killed by wild animals? It might, or it might not. There was nothing to prove that Sanaya hadn't vanished into thin air or sunk without a trace into the earth.

"I can hope so," said Neena. "I cannot wish even on Sanaya the death she would receive from those of Trawn."

"No," said Blade. "You are not eaten up with vengeance, as she would be in your place." He kissed her and blew out the candle. After a moment he felt her flowing

150

against him in the darkness, warm in the chill of the forest night. After another moment, he found himself responding as he always did.

It was the fourteenth night after the test in the arena and Queen Sanaya's flight into the forest.

Lord Desgo reined in his meytan and raised his hand in signal for those behind him to do the same. Silence fell over the forest as a score of six-legged beasts ceased their steady trot. Absentmindedly, Lord Desgo scratched his mount between its long golden-furred ears, then swung himself down out of the saddle. The warriors behind him did the same, then gathered around him.

"I think I need say what we are to do only once more. Capture the Princess Neena and at least one of the Kaireens at the workshop. Slay the tall man Blade and every other living thing in sight. Then burn all that can burn, and depart with the prisoners. You all have firemakers?" The warriors nodded and patted the pouches at their belts.

"Good." Two more warriors stepped forward out of the shadows. Between them they led Queen Sanaya, naked, shivering, and with her hands tied behind her back. She cringed as she became aware of all the warriors' eyes running up and down her body.

Desgo smiled grimly. Sanaya was not feigning her shame before the warriors. That only made her disguise all the more perfect. The bound hands and the nudity marked her as a prisoner, but in her heart and soul Sanaya was no longer a prisoner.

Instead, she was Desgo's ally. Or rather, she thought herself his ally. With her guiding him, Desgo would tonight destroy Draad's secret weapons, slay Prince Blade, and begin his vengeance against Princess Neena. Then in a few days he would order the waiting army of Trawn forward. It would pour into Draad, killing every warrior who stood against it, but as few others as possible.

Lord Desgo had no tenderness for the women and children of Draad. He had only a coldly calculating desire to make them grateful to him and to Queen Sanaya for sparing them. He would be ruling them with her beside him, and soon. After such a victory as he would win, King Furzun could hardly make anyone else viceroy over the newly conquered lands.

And after that? The visions of what might be were even more enticing. With Queen Sanaya to advise him, he could certainly devise ways of winning and keeping the loyalty of the people of Draad. The emerald mines would give him wealth, wealth to reward any warrior of Draad or Trawn who would follow his standard, wealth also to reward those nobles and merchants of Trawnom-Driba who had already promised to be his allies.

Over the years, he would forge his warriors and allies into an army, an army standing ready like a weapon for his hand to wield. In the end, he would wield it against King Furzun. Furzun would die in his own prison chambers, and King Desgo would rule Trawn and Draad and all the lands and forests of Gleor!

With the favor of the gods, he would do it. He would have prayed for that favor, except that this was no time for prayer and Desgo was not a praying man in any case. Loud prayers would earn less favor from the gods than shrewd blows with a sword.

He took Sanaya from the hands of the two guards and lifted her onto the neck of the meytan. Then he scrambled back up into the saddle behind her. The other warriors of the raiding party did the same. All of them carried swords, bows, and throwing spears; five of them led stolofs. One of the stolofs chittered briefly, and was promptly silenced by a spear butt rapped across its head. Desgo raised his hand, then pointed forward into the darkness and dug in his spurs.

The gods would be with them tonight. Desgo was certain of that. The warriors and the stolofs and the riding meytans were all picked and trained, the best available. The workshop was guarded weakly, if at all. The mountain clans might patrol the forests all around, to be sure. They could not see in the dark like a meytan, nor stand against stolofs.

Guided by Queen Sanaya and mounted as they were,

the raiders would be on their enemy before any alarm could be given. Then it would be fire, death, bonds of captivity for Neena, and flight into the darkness faster than any of Draad could follow!

Princess Neena had no more than an hour of freedom left. Prince Blade had no more than an hour of life.

Chapter 26

Blade awoke in the darkness with Neena's warm body curled against him. That wasn't what had awakened him, though. Something else had penetrated into his sleep and brought him out of it. He sat up in bed and listened. The darkness around him seemed utterly silent. He'd heard something—he was sure of it. He had the instincts of a hunting animal for the dangerous or the unusual, instincts that seldom let him down.

Then a sound came out of the darkness, faint and far away, muffled by distance and by the forest. It was also a sound that shouldn't have been heard anywhere for many miles around. It was unmistakably the chittering of a stolof.

Blade rolled out of bed and began pulling on his clothes and weapons. The noises he made awakened Neena. She sat up in bed, pulling the blankets around her against the chill of the night air on her bare skin, and stared sleepily at Blade. She did not have his knack of being fully alert the moment she awoke. He was about to shake her when the chittering came out of the night again. It was just as unmistakable this time, and it was closer.

Neena leaped out of bed as if she'd received an electric shock and began dressing. Blade finished belting on his sword and hurried into the room where the three assistants slept. He woke them quickly and silently.

"Raiders from Trawn approach. Arm yourselves, but stay here and guard our comrade." He pointed to the door of the room where Kulo tossed in his pain-ridden sleep. "Don't move out unless I call, or you have to. Whatever you do, don't let yourselves be captured alive."

The three young men stared at him, then scrambled out of their beds. They might not understand exactly what he'd said, but they understood his tone of voice. Certainly they understood what being captured by raiders from Trawn might mean.

Blade was sure they would do their best. He turned and dashed back to the bedroom, where Neena was now fully armed and dressed except for her tunic. Blade passed on without stopping, heading for the main door. He wanted to get out into the courtyard, where he would have fighting room and a clear view of what was going on. He also wanted to call out and start the alarm on its way to the main camp of the stolof killers two miles away.

As Blade put his hand on the bar of the door, a wild scream came out of the darkness. "Raiders, raiders! They come with sto—" The words ended in another sort of scream, one with agony as well as terror in it. A moment of silence, then a chorus of chittering that sounded like a whole herd of stolofs, an unmistakably human war cry, stolof-whistles, and the pad-pad-pad of dozens of soft hooves on the earth.

Neena stared at Blade. "They must have come in on meytans, to come in so fast like this. The gods only know what they may be bringing with them!"

"The gods won't get the word to us in time," snapped Blade. He kicked the door open so hard that it nearly flew off its hinges. Then he snatched up a loaded sprayer with one hand and a sack of throwing pots with the other. Behind him Neena grabbed up her two spears and her threebo, tucked them under one arm, then picked up a sprayer with her free hand. Both of them dashed through the open door and out into the courtyard.

As they reached the open, another sentry died outside the walls with a horrible gurgling scream. Again the chorus of chitterings sounded, as well as heavy grunting that must have been the meytans. Something heavy crashed against the outside of the main gate. Blade saw the logs shiver and pieces of bark fall to the ground.

154

He also heard other shouts—"Raiders, raiders, raiders of Trawn. Come, come, come!" The clansmen and warriors on alert were doing their job, shouting the warning from one to another down the hill to the camp. When word reached the camp, King Embor would be on his way with enough trained stolof killers to swamp the raiders. How long would that take?

Again the gate shivered. This time one of the crosspieces split apart with a sharp crack. The gate was designed to keep out thieves and the wild animals of the mountain forests, not half-ton stolofs, charging meytans, or battering rams wielded by warriors of Trawn.

Crash! A third blow, and this time one of the logs of the gate twisted out of position and sagged inward. Through the gap Blade could see a confused, churning mass of nightmare shapes—stolofs, the great floppy-eared heads of the meytans, the helmets of warriors. The foul smell of stolofs reached Blade on the night breeze, so strong that he gasped and coughed to clear it out of his throat and nostrils.

He heard the *chuff* of an arrow sinking into flesh, and one of the warrior's heads twisted and jerked and sagged out of sight. A moment later a stolof chittered hysterically, closer to the forest. Another hideous scream came, along with the crunching of mandibles as they closed on a human body.

Blade swore. Mountain clansmen were dying out there, perhaps needlessly, and if so it was his fault. He had deliberately not armed the clansmen on guard with sprayers, so they would not be tempted to attack raiders instead of just giving warning. He should have remembered how the mountain men hated those of Trawn, and how none of them would hold back from a battle, regardless of what weapons they held. He had made a mistake.

Well, there was a good chance he would pay for that mistake himself, and Neena along with him. The alarm would certainly bring warriors by the score up the hill within a few minutes. That would be soon enough to save the workshop. But he and Neena were another matter. Draad would have its victory—Blade was sure of that.

155

But he was not so sure that he and Neena would live to see it.

At least they would get that chance he'd hoped for, to test the distilled sleeping water on live stolofs!

Something sputtered and hissed outside. A sickly yellow glow lit up the churning shapes beyond the gate, making them look even more ghastly than before. Then something trailing yellow flame and sparks came flying over the wall. It struck the roof of the workshop, bounced, and rolled off onto the ground. It lay there sputtering and sizzling and spitting more flames and more sparks and puffing out foul-smelling dark greasy smoke.

Blade swore and slapped Neena on the shoulder. "Run back inside to the assistants. Tell them to get the fire buckets filled and ready, but not to come outside. Those bastards are trying to burn us out." Neena dropped her weapons, turned, and dashed back into the workshop.

As she disappeared, three arrows came whistling down from the top of the wall and smacked into the workshop just above the doorway. Blade looked up to see that three of the enemy warriors had climbed the outside of the wall and were straddling it precariously. They were already nocking fresh arrows to their bows.

Blade caught up one of Neena's spears and hurled it. It smashed squarely into the mouth of one of the raiders and up into his brain in a spray of blood and smashed teeth. He threw up his hands and toppled backward off the wall without a sound. A second warrior jerked, lost his balance, and toppled forward with a scream. He fell head first and afterward lay without moving, his neck bent at an impossible angle. The third warrior loosed his arrow, but it smacked into the ground well to one side of Blade and skittered away into the darkness.

Before the warrior could nock another arrow, stolof-whistles sounded outside the gate. So did the chittering of the creatures, louder and fiercer than before. They surged forward against the gate and two more logs fell clear, one of them splitting in two as it fell. A spear sailed in through the wider gap and Blade had to dart to one side to avoid being hit.

156

Then with a tremendous cracking and crunching the gate caved in completely, and the way into the compound was open. For a moment it was solidly blocked by the mass of stolofs, meytans, and warriors crowded in the gateway. That was a moment that Blade used well. It was a moment when all his enormous strength and lightning reflexes were turned to one purpose—killing. It was a moment when he was in fact nothing but a killing machine.

Blade hurled the second spear at the last archer on the wall, and hit him just as he was loosing another arrow. The arrow sailed off into the darkness and the archer sailed backward off the wall, the spear through his stomach. Before the man hit the ground Blade whirled, snatched up a pot of sleeping water, and hurled it into the mob in the gateway.

He aimed at the head of the nearest stolof, and his aim was flawless. The pot flew straight and smashed into the creature just above the three eyes. Sleeping water sluiced down over its head and over its breathing holes. It chittered frantically, then fell silent. Slowly it tilted over to the left as all the legs on one side gave way. Then the rest of its legs folded up and it lay down. It was not dead, for its mandibles still clicked feebly, but it was a dead weight, squarely in the path of the other attackers.

Blade went flat as two arrows whistled by, then sprang up with his sprayer in both hands. The range was long but he did not need to aim precisely. He swung the sprayer back and forth across the gateway, firing steady bursts until it was empty. A second stolof stopped dead, chittering steadily. It did not collapse, but no amount of whistling or yelling by the warriors could get it moving again.

One of the warriors lost his patience and scrambled forward over the collapsed stolof, sword in one hand and spear raised to throw in the other. As he thrust his head up and forward, Blade hit him squarely in the mouth with a jet from the sprayer. The warrior's weapons dropped from his suddenly limp fingers. He collapsed facedown on top of the stolof, then rolled off onto the ground.

Another warrior sprang up on top of the fallen stolof, a

lighted firemaker swinging in one hand. He hurled it straight into the nearest window of the workshop. Blade yelled for fire buckets. Answering shouts came from inside.

Then Neena dashed out into the courtyard. In her hands was a bow, an arrow already nocked to the string. She took aim and shot, and the warrior who'd thrown the firemaker screamed as an arrow suddenly sprouted in his left eye. He did not go down, but he turned and reeled away, still screaming.

The man's screams seemed to paralyze all of his comrades and their animals. For a moment nothing moved and not a weapon was raised in the crowd at the gateway. Blade and Neena could look out clearly, to see Lord Desgo ride up on a meytan, holding a naked Queen Sanaya in front of him.

Neena shrieked like a madwoman and snatched frantically for an arrow. As if in answer to her scream, angry shouts and war cries exploded from the forest. Then came the sound of scores of running feet and the crackling of scores of men pushing through bushes. The stolof killers were moving into the attack.

Neena shot, the twang of her bowstring lost in the uproar. Her arrow flashed toward Lord Desgo, but the nobleman's reflexes were even quicker. He ducked, jerking Sanaya across in front of him as a shield. The arrow sank into her body just below the left breast. She shrieked, clawing at the arrow, then shrieked again as Desgo heaved her off the back of the meytan and dug in his spurs.

Neena slung her bow and she and Blade leaped forward. They sprang up onto the back of the fallen stolof, facing two warriors. Neena whipped her threebo up and over and down on one man's shoulder, and his sword arm dropped limply. The threebo scythed in a deadly arc from the left, and the man's head snapped violently to one side as temple and jaw caved in.

Blade's man tried to run. Blade thrust him through the neck from behind, so that the sword went through the man's spine going in and through his windpipe coming

158

out. Blade jerked his sword free and let the man topple.

Then the stolof killers of Draad swarmed out of the forest and charged past the gate. Some of them threw away their sprayers and drew clubs and axes as they saw how few stolofs there were to kill. One team of four faced a live and healthy stolof and its master, and Blade shouted for joy as he saw them put their training to work.

One dashed around to engage the stolof's master, stone-headed axe against sword. Two others stood ready to attack the stolof, and the last raised his sprayer. As he took aim, the stolof launched a ribbon. The ribbon fell on his shoulder and one arm, but he did not flinch. He rammed in the plunger and the sleeping water jetted out in a precisely aimed spray and fell on the stolof's breathing holes. The stolof's master whistled, trying to make it rear and jerk the sprayer man off his feet. The stolof would not obey. It only stood there, quivering and chittering softly. The sprayer man fired again. At the same moment the stolof's master thrust his sword through his opponent's belly, and died as the other's axe crashed down on his skull. Then the remaining two warriors of Draad charged in, sinking an axe and a spear into the stolof's eyes. It chittered one last time, hissed, sprayed yellowish mist and foam, then collapsed and lay still. Blade shouted again.

By now all of the men and beasts of the raiding party were either dead, caught, or fleeing for their lives. Blade caught a glimpse of Lord Desgo pounding away toward the safety of the woods, alone. Neena saw this too, and unslung her bow. It was a long shot, made harder by the darkness and the fast-moving target, but Neena's eye was deadly and her aim nearly as good. Blade saw Lord Desgo jump high, nearly leaping out of his saddle, then clap his hands to his buttocks, where Neena's arrow stood out like a suddenly sprouted tail. Blade threw back his head and roared with laughter as Lord Desgo vanished into the dark. Then he threw his arms around Neena, and they laughed and shouted and pounded each other on the back and danced each other around in a circle.

They were still doing that when they realized that the

battle's uproar was fading away around them. They stepped apart and Blade told Neena to go seek out her father. He himself turned and went back into the workshop compound.

There he found everything surprisingly well in hand. Two of the raiders had tried to climb over the rear wall, to make a diversion. One had fallen off and knocked himself out. One of the assistants had ambushed the other in a dark alley between two sheds and hit him over the head with a bucket. Both men were still alive, and Blade gave orders to keep them that way. A little interrogation would do nobody (except possibly the prisoners) any harm. The firemaker had done some damage to the living quarters, but none to anything else. Blade looked in briefly on Kulo, who had somehow managed to stay asleep through the whole battle, and went back outside.

By this time Neena had found her father. Both of them were standing over a sprawled form on the ground. It was Queen Sanaya, and she was not a pleasant sight. The arrow had pierced a lung, and then she had broken several bones being flung down from Desgo's mount. After that, meytans, stolofs, and running men of both sides had trampled her. She was covered with dirt and blood, and there was only a very little bit of life still in her. As she realized that people were standing over her, she turned her head and tried to speak, but all that came out were small bubbles of blood.

King Embor sighed. "Have her taken to a safe place and given all possible care by Kaireens."

"It will do no good, father," said Neena.

Embor sighed. "True enough, daughter. But she was once my wife and my queen." He turned away, calling to his guards.

Queen Sanaya died just before dawn, and soon after that so did the last of the prisoners. Neena had taken charge of their interrogation, and she had not been gentle. She had learned much that would be useful.

"Desgo and the other raiders and scouts come from an army that is indeed nearly upon us," she said. "The last the prisoners knew of it, it was only four days' march from the Mountains of Hoga and under orders to stay there until Lord Desgo returned."

"How large is it?" said Embor.

"All the prisoners spoke of at least twenty thousand warriors and a thousand stolofs. None of them knew too much, and the one who seemed to know the most died the soonest."

"Perhaps you should have gone easier on him," said Blade. Neena tossed her head with a snort of contempt at the idea of "going easy" on anyone from Trawn.

"In any case," she went on, "we shall have our war with Trawn sooner than we expected. Within weeks perhaps, within a month or two certainly. Lord Desgo is disgraced, and damn the gods that he is not dead! He will want vengeance for that arrow that I put into his rear end, and soon. He will come to us. We can do best by gathering our strength and waiting for him to come."

There was nothing Blade or King Embor could say against that strategy. It was not only the best for Draad, it was nearly the only one. They would be fighting against heavy odds, even with their new and now proven weapons.

"Very well," said King Embor. "We shall do that. Meanwhile we shall gather all the chiefs and principal warriors, and give Sanaya a proper funeral."

Neena's eyebrows shot up, her face darkened, and she would undoubtedly have exploded if Blade hadn't put a hand firmly over her mouth. King Embor shook his head.

"It shall be as I say, daughter. We know what Queen Sanaya did, the three of us, but few others, and they can be kept silent. She lived foolishly and died shamefully, but let that be the end of her dishonor. I will not add to it, nor will I shame her clan, not now of all times!"

Neena looked as if she still wanted to protest, but King Embor and Blade both stared her down and her protest died unspoken.

King Embor was right, Blade had to admit. Whatever Queen Sanaya might have done, she had in the end died without doing any real harm. There was an end to the affair and an end to her, and there was nothing more to be said about either.

Chapter 27

King Embor's warriors scoured the forests around the workshop for three days. By the end of the third day they knew that every one of the raiders was either dead or had fled beyond the Mountains of Hoga. The next move was up to Lord Desgo.

Blade realized that the timing of Trawn's invasion might depend on something as simple as the condition of Lord Desgo's wounded buttocks. Would he insist on waiting until he could again comfortably lead his warriors from the saddle of a meytan? Or would he be willing to be carried into battle, seated on cushions in a litter or perhaps even lying facedown? It was amusing to speculate on the question, and also quite pointless.

What was *not* pointless was to assemble all the warriors Draad could put into the field and train them, train them, train them! Blade started putting in eighteen-hour days again, putting the warriors through one maneuver after another. He was not worried about overtraining them. Lord Desgo would certainly strike long before a single warrior of Draad would have time to get impatient or bored with Blade's training. Desgo would also strike with at least a two-to-one superiority in numbers, and by no means all of his warriors would have two left feet. In an army of twenty thousand, drawn from a people who loved violence if not necessarily war, there would be a good many men who knew their business. Draad could only hope to survive if its warriors took every advantage and every bit of training they could get.

Day followed day. The sense that something was about to happen hung over Draad's army and its leaders like the mists on the Mountains of Hoga. For Blade one day began to blend into another in an endless, unvarying, and increasingly monotonous succession.

Still more days. Now the scouts of the mountain clans were moving out beyond the Mountains of Hoga, watching Lord Desgo's army. Some obeyed their orders and lived to bring or send back word of the enemy's strength and position. Others disobeyed, tried to launch attacks of their own, and did not come back.

It was just under a month after the raid when the scouts reported that Desgo's army was on the march. The first reports had it marching north. King Embor was all for moving Draad's assembled army in the same direction.

Blade had other ideas. "That is what Desgo will be expecting us to do. Therefore we should not do it."

"What do you suggest, Blade?" said the king. His eyes were red, his hair grayer than when Blade had first met him, and his voice edged with both exhaustion and anger. "Is there anything else to do, that will not let Desgo come through the passes and burn and kill in Draad? I do not want to live to see that!"

"None of us do, father," said Neena. "Think that, and let my husband speak."

Blade continued. "What I suggest is that we march our army *south,* toward the Pass of Kitos. It is the largest of the mountain passes and the closest one to the emerald mines. Desgo can march his whole army through it quickly. Elsewhere he would have to use two or three passes, or else send his army through very slowly. Both would be dangerous, since we could attack him before he could reunite his army."

Blade's finger stabbed at the deerskin map on the table in front of them. "Also, on our side of the Pass of Kitos is a stretch of open land nearly a day's march wide. There is plenty of room there for Desgo's army to maneuver and fight its battle as a single force. Anywhere else in Draad, he would risk fighting with his army split up and not knowing the land, against an enemy who knows the land very well. Desgo will see this open ground as the best place to fight his battle, and sooner or later he will come there. Why not by the most direct route?

163

"I agree," said Neena. "Lord Desgo deserves fifty filthy names. But he is not a fool, and anyone who thinks otherwise certainly is!"

"Very well," said the king. "We shall take the risks. Certainly it gives us a better hope of a victory that will give us many years of peace. But I shall pray to the gods with all my strength, Blade, that Lord Desgo is only as wise as you think he is, and no wiser!"

Lord Desgo's army marched north, with Draad's scouts watching it. Draad's army marched south, unwatched. At Blade's suggestion King Embor had all the passes patrolled so that a cockroach couldn't have gotten through, let alone an enemy scouting party. Those patrols added up to a good many warriors who would not be available for the battle in the south. Yet they would not be wasted, if they gave Draad the advantage of surprise.

Those weren't all the warriors Blade was planning to detach. When Lord Desgo's army was well through the Pass of Kitos—*if* it came that way—another force of warriors would slip into position on either side of the pass. They could strike at Desgo's rear, or ambush his army as it tried to retreat from Draad.

Eventually they reached the forests on the edge of the open land around the Pass of Kitos. The ambush party split off and marched up into the mountains on either side of the pass. The rest of Draad's warriors settled into concealed camps in the forest, with nothing left to do but wait.

They had to wait ten days. King Embor seemed to age a year during each of those days, gnawed by fear that he had doomed ten thousand of his people by following Blade's advice. Blade and Neena found it best to avoid him.

Then on the eleventh day the word came through—Lord Desgo's army had swung about, and was approaching the western end of the Pass of Kitos. On the thirteenth day it entered the pass. By evening on the fifteenth day it was camped on the open land to the east of the pass.

164

That was the evening when Blade and Neena climbed a tall tree on the edge of the forest and looked out upon their enemy. The campfires of Desgo's army made a long ragged crescent across three miles of land, a flickering orange crescent blurred by the rising mists of evening.

"They will be nearly three to one against what we will have on the field tomorrow," said Neena. "I hope fighting in the open against such odds is not the kind of folly the gods hate, so that they will punish us for it."

"It could be," Blade admitted. "I would not be thinking of it under other conditions. But you know all that I have taught our warriors that they did not know before and which will be a surprise to Desgo. Our warriors are also strong and well-rested, while Desgo's men have marched fast and far on sore feet and growling stomachs. We will move faster than they can tomorrow. I think the gods will not call our battle a folly."

"I hope not," said Neena. Then she smiled, "Shall we go back down, or would you take me here, in the branches with the wind in our ears?"

"I think we will go back down," said Blade with a chuckle. "I would not care to go down in the chronicles of Draad as the warrior who on the night before his greatest battle fell out of a tall tree while embracing his woman and smashed himself into small pieces on the ground!"

The next day, Blade fought his battle.

Lord Desgo formed his army in a wide shallow line a mile wide but only a few ranks deep. This formation had worked well enough in the past against opponents with no answer to the stolofs. It might not work so well now.

"Lord Desgo probably knows that as well as we do," said Blade. "But he has not had time to train his men in any new tactics, so he will not try them. If he did, his army would fall into confusion and he would be even worse off. He will try what has worked in the past, and hope for the favor of the gods and enough skill and courage in his warriors." He did not add that Draad would have to hope for exactly the same things in order to be

165

sure of victory. Neena probably knew that just as well as he did.

It was a misty morning. Blade counted on that for some help. The mist was not thick enough to permit real surprises, but it would be useful for the first of his planned tricks.

The army of Draad marched out of the woods in the same wide thin line as the enemy. To stretch a mile, Draad's warriors had to be spread even thinner than Trawn's. Blade's first trick was intended to conceal that fact.

The warriors with regular weapons formed the first rank. Behind them moved a thin second line, all the stolof killers together. With each of them marched a helper—wife, concubine, trusted servant, sometimes a son or even a daughter. These helpers carried the extra sprayers, the heavy sacks of throwing pots, everything that would weigh down or slow down a stolof killer. When the time came for them to charge, the stolof killers would dash forward like black stalkers on their prey.

Behind the stolof killers came a whole mass of people. Every man for miles around who could put one foot in front of another was there, and a good many women and older children. There were gray-bearded grandfathers, youths just learning weapons, craftsmen of all kinds, workers from the emerald mines under their overseers, wives, midwives, and courtesans. There were nearly ten thousand of them, outnumbering the actual warriors Blade and Embor had brought to the field.

Perhaps five hundred of these ten thousand could use some sort of a weapon with any skill. Lord Desgo wouldn't know that. As Draad's army marched out of the morning mists toward him, it would look twice as strong as it really was. Desgo would lose any hope of overwhelming the enemy by sheer weight of numbers and become cautious. By the time Desgo discovered that he'd been tricked, it hopefully wouldn't matter. Blade intended for the nobleman to have too much else on his mind!

King Embor marched with the warriors of the front rank, Blade with the stolof killers, Neena among the civilians to the rear. Neena also kept an eye on the dozen captured meytans that were being led forward, carefully concealed among the civilians. They also had their place in Blade's plans.

The army of Draad marched forward. On the level ground, the warriors and stolof killers were able to keep an impressively precise formation. The Brigade of Guards on parade in London could hardly have done any better. Precision like that was something new, something unknown in Gleor—and facing anything unknown was likely to unsettle Desgo or his warriors or both.

Just over a mile ahead, the army of Trawn slowly appeared out of the mist, already drawn up in its battle formation. King Embor, Blade, and Neena shouted orders, and the army of Draad came to a stop, just outside bowshot from the enemy's line. Silence fell on the field, and nothing moved except for the gentle eddying of the mist as the morning breezes began to blow.

Lord Desgo sat on his meytan in the rear of his army's line and stared out at the enemy.

"More of them than I'd expected," said one of the warriors of his household.

Desgo nodded. "We're not going to simply roll forward and stamp them into the ground." He turned to a messenger. "Tell the Master of the Stolofs to bring his men and beasts forward, ready for a full attack."

Another of Desgo's household frowned and spoke up boldly. "Sire, we have here most of the war-trained stolofs of Trawn. You say the enemy has a weapon to slay or cripple the stolofs. Yet—"

"You doubt my war wisdom?" said Desgo, his voice suddenly cool and his hand on the hilt of his dagger. The other man shook his head, although his expression didn't match the gesture at all.

"No, sire. I wonder, though, about running too great risks with the stolofs."

"We will be running no risks," snapped Desgo. "I saw Blade's weapon work against half a dozen stolofs. We shall not see it work so well against a thousand."

167

"The stolofs are coming forward," said King Embor, striding up to Blade. "That means an attack after their usual fashion."

"Good," said Blade. "Lord Desgo can go on doing things the usual way as long as he pleases—or as long as he can."

King Embor nodded and strode away, back to his position in the front rank. He looked like a man whose nerves were being plucked at with red-hot pincers. Blade did not blame him. Once the battle was joined, the fate of Draad would probably be decided in less than an hour. That was why Blade had spent all those days training the warriors of Draad to move at top speed.

Hopefully they would be moving faster than Lord Desgo could think.

The stolof-whistles seemed to be blowing continuously in the enemy's lines now. They sounded like an immense cage of oversized and not very musical birds.

Blade looked up and down the line of stolof killers. Some of them had gone as pale as the brown-skinned warriors of Draad could go. Many were licking their lips or shuffling their sandaled feet. Blade did not blame them. For all the power of their new weapons, there was still some power in the ancient fear of the stolofs, the monsters that had given Trawn mastery of so many battlefields for so many generations.

With luck, that fear would die today, along with most of the stolofs.

In twos and threes and half dozens and dozens the stolofs crept out through Trawn's line into open view. Their numbers mounted up—two hundred, three hundred, five hundred, seven hundred. More of the stolof killers turned pale.

It looked as though Desgo was going to launch a simple attack, coming straight in and hoping to overpower by terror and sheer weight of numbers. Two or three warriors would be advancing with each stolof, and together they were supposed to break Draad's line apart. Then Desgo would launch the rest of his army on the broken formation, and that would be the battle.

168

Still the stolofs came out, until there must have been nearly a thousand of them. Blade neither turned pale nor shuffled his feet, but his mind was working furiously. This must be not only every stolof in Desgo's army, but damned near every war-trained stolof in Trawn! Destroying them all would make this a day Trawn would never forget, whatever else happened. Desgo was gambling his stolofs in pursuit of an easy victory; he might end up giving that easy victory to Draad.

But first Draad's stolof killers had to stand up to a thousand of the monsters, and beat them back or destroy them. That was not going to be easy. Blade found himself even more sympathetic toward those stolof killers who had by now turned the color of dirty bedsheets. So far none of them was looking over his shoulder, picking out a safe route to the rear. The courage of the warriors of Draad might falter, but Blade doubted if he would see it fail.

The stolof-whistles fell silent. There were odd flurries of movement as some of the warriors in the attack formation shifted position. Then those horribly unmusical trumpets of Trawn sounded.

Blade shouted so that everyone could hear him. "If that is how they play now, can you imagine how they'll sound after we've beaten them?" It was not a particularly good joke, but it cut like a sharp knife through the tension among the stolof killers. A roar of laughter went up and down the line, and only died when the enemy's trumpets sounded again, this time sounding the charge for both warriors and stolofs.

The enemy line moved slowly forward, the warriors matching their stride to the lumbering pace of the stolofs. Some tried to urge their stolofs to a faster pace; none succeeded.

Three hundred yards. Two hundred. A hundred and fifty. A hundred and twenty. Blade and King Embor kept their eyes fixed on the approaching enemy. When they reached one hundred yards—

They did. Trumpeters and drummers sent signals racing along Draad's battle line. Almost in a single motion,

169

all the archers in the front racks nocked arrows, raised their bows, aimed, and shot. Two thousand arrows flashed toward the approaching line, whistling like a winter sleet storm. Then the whistling of the arrows gave way to screams and hisses as they struck home in men and stolofs.

The stolofs were nearly invulnerable to the arrows from Draad's bows. The warriors were another matter. They wore tough leather armor from throat to groin, but there were plenty of faces, arms and legs exposed to the storm of arrows. Plenty of those arrows found targets. Warriors of Trawn staggered about, waving bleeding arms, clapping hands to bloody thighs, screaming as they tried to pick arrows out of their eyes or faces. Not too many of them went down, but a good many of them lagged behind or blundered about wildly.

Then the second flight of arrows whistled down on the advancing line. The range was closer now, and more of the arrows struck vulnerable spots. Some of those that struck the leather armor struck hard enough to penetrate, not fatally but painfully. Blade heard many more screams, a great many curses, and angry hissing from the stolofs. Their armor was as tough as ever, but the sheer number of arrows coming at them was bound to produce a few lucky shots. Several stolofs were going down, arrows sprouting among their eyes. Many others seemed to be slowing down or moving uncertainly.

A thousand warriors of Trawn were now maimed or at least hurting. The archers of Draad nocked and drew for a third flight of arrows. Before the arrows came down, most of the warriors darted behind their stolofs, crouching low. Most of the arrows bounced harmlessly off the armor of the stolofs or the thick rounded helmets of the warriors. Few did any real harm that Blade could see.

That was perfectly all right with him. Hiding behind their stolofs, the warriors could not guide the creatures well. The stolofs were slow to obey or respond to anything or anyone they could not see in front of them. And the warriors could no longer stand between their stolofs and any attackers.

Blade looked along the line of stolof killers and raised his hands in a signal. A thousand fighting men scooped throwing pots out of bags with one hand and raised their sprayers with the other. There were still pale faces in the line, but the tension was gone. They had seen the charge of the stolofs already blunted by Blade's innovation of massed archery. Now they confidently expected to smash the charge entirely with the Prince's new sleeping water.

The fourth flight of arrows whistled across the narrowing gap between the two lines. A few of the braver warriors went down, those who hadn't ducked for cover behind the stolofs. A couple of dozen stolofs also went down. That was all—the vulnerable spots on a stolof were too small to make good targets even at close range. But every stolof that stumbled and sagged and dropped out of line made the line still more ragged. Instead of crashing into Draad's warriors as a solid, irresistible mass, Trawn's attack was coming forward as an increasingly ragged and disorderly mob, stolofs and warriors all mixed up together.

The archers pulled arrows for a fifth flight out of their quivers, but held their fire. Blade raised his hands still higher, until everyone in the line of stolof killers could see his signal. Then he flung his arms downward. Trumpets blared again, and the whole line surged forward.

They dashed up through the gaps between the archers and other warriors of the front ranks and out into the open. The warriors of Trawn reacted swiftly, springing out from behind their stolofs, swords and spears held ready for battle.

As the warriors of Trawn burst out of cover, every one of the running stolof killers bent forward at the waist without breaking stride. A few of them lost their balance and sprawled on the grass, scattering pots and sandals as they rolled over and over. A moment later the archers of Draad loosed their fifth flight of arrows, straight over the heads of their running comrades, straight into the faces of the warriors of Trawn. At close range the arrows stabbed through leather armor into hearts and lungs, stomachs and vital arteries. Hundreds of warriors went down as if

171

someone had turned a death ray on them, and several dozen stolofs also folded up and slumped to the ground.

This had been the riskiest part of Blade's whole battle plan. If the archers had aimed only a little bit low, they could have wiped out hundreds of the stolof killers and very few of the enemy. Blade could see they had aimed well. The enemy's ranks were gaping, while only a few of the stolof killers and a score or so of the attendants running behind them were down. That was all Blade had time to see before the charge of the stolof killers struck the enemy's line.

Most of the stolofs' masters were either too badly wounded or too surprised to order their charges to launch ribbons. A good many ribbons went out, nonetheless, as the stolofs got it into their tiny brains that something ought to be done about all those men running toward them. Most of those ribbons struck; the stolofs were good shots to the end. The stolofs who had a victim on the end of their ribbons reared back as they'd been trained to do. The stolof killers who hadn't been caught threw their pots and opened up with their sprayers. Then the battle dissolved in a screaming, hissing, swirling chaos so complete that Blade himself couldn't keep track of anything going on more than six feet from him.

He saw a ribbon coming at him, darted aside, and saw the ribbon slap against the cheek of a girl loaded with a stolof killer's extra pots and sprayers. She screamed and went down, her bag bursting open and scattering pots across the grass. Some broke, some didn't. The stolof killer snatched up one of the unbroken pots and hurled it at the stolof. It struck the creature just as it reared, dragging the girl forward and making her scream again. Sleeping water poured down over the breathing holes, and the stolof seemed to freeze and stand still, reared back on its hind legs, forelegs in the air, mandibles clicking steadily. The stolof killer bent to slash the ribbon with his bone knife. As he did so, a warrior with a spear ran past him, straight at the stolof. The man drove his spear with all his strength into the vulnerable part of the stolof's belly. Then he sprang clear of the spray of foul-smelling yellow

172

fluid, as the creature quivered all over and collapsed. An enemy warrior sprang up from behind the fallen creature, leaped up on top of it, and attacked the man from Draad, sword against spear.

Blade dashed forward. A single leap carried him up onto the stolof's back beside the enemy warrior, and a single slash from his sword took off the man's head. The spouting corpse toppled off the stolof in one direction, and Blade sprang down in another. Before the warrior he'd saved even had a chance to thank him, a sudden surge forward by the enemy drove them apart. Blade found himself surrounded by stolofs who were jammed too close together to fire their ribbons. A moment later they came to a stop, too crowded together to even move.

Blade ducked in and out between the thick green and golden legs as if he was running through a forest. At unexpected moments he popped out from under the stolofs, sword in one hand and spear in the other. In those moments warriors of Trawn died screaming or choking in their own blood. Blade must have killed eight or ten without taking a single scratch. Then stolof-whistles blew and the creatures began moving backward. Blade ducked under a last one, stabbed it in the belly, ran across in front of another one to thrust his spear into its eyes, then broke out into the open.

As he did a fresh wave of Draad's warriors came in, more spearmen and some of the archers as well. The archers dropped into cover behind the dead stolofs that now littered the ground and began picking off any enemy they could hit without risk of hitting a friend. The spearmen pushed forward, stabbing wounded or stunned stolofs and dying or crippled enemy warriors as they came to them. Blade stepped back through the advancing line, and for the first time in quite a while got a clear view of the battle.

The main formation of Desgo's army was still intact and unmoving, unable to see or perhaps understand what was happening to the stolofs' attack. What was happening to that attack was quite simply a massacre. Two-thirds of the warriors and stolofs were already dead or dying.

The rest were too paralyzed by fear or surprise or sleeping water to make any effort to flee or defend themselves. It was only a matter of time before they also died.

It was also only a matter of time before Lord Desgo and his commanders recovered from the shock of seeing their stolofs and several thousand of their best warriors massacred before their eyes. That was why speed was so vital for Blade's tactics. He had to deliver his second and finishing stroke to Desgo's army before the enemy recovered enough to realize what was about to happen to them.

Blade turned and sprinted back toward the rear, angling toward the left of his own army. King Embor could and would do all that was necessary to push the main battle. It was time for him and Neena to lead their own attack.

Blade slowed down as he approached the mass of civilians. He didn't want to be seen running by people who might not clearly understand why he was doing so. That was the way panics and routs got started and victorious armies could disintegrate in the moment of victory.

Blade trotted through the civilians, ignoring the cheers and the hands reaching out to touch him, and reached the meytans. Neena was already in the saddle. He swung himself up onto the back of his meytan and thrust his feet firmly into the stirrups.

Lord Desgo felt sweat trickling under his helmet. The sun had just cleared the treetops to the east and was only beginning to thin out the mist over the battlefield. Desgo's sweat was the cold sweat of a man who has just seen his army's main striking force destroyed in ten minutes. Desgo found it hard to keep his hands from shaking as he held the reins of his meytan or his voice from shaking as he gave his orders.

It was hard to see exactly what Draad's army was doing, what with the mist and the slaughter of the stolofs that was still going on. It looked as if they were extending their line, perhaps trying to push their flanks out beyond his. That made no sense to Desgo. They couldn't get anything out of that maneuver, not without twice as many

174

men as they had. Still, flank attacks were sometimes possible. It would be well to extend his own line to match Draad's, even though it would make the line thinner than he liked. Yet that was certainly the least dangerous course of action. There was nothing Draad could do to break through his line that wouldn't give him plenty of warning.

The uproar to Blade's right faded as the last of the stolofs died and the last of the enemy warriors either died or fled back to their own lines. Barely a hundred of them made it.

Desgo's first attack had been not only defeated but destroyed. Half the danger to Draad had died with the stolofs. Perhaps the sensible thing to do now was to disengage, hoping that Desgo would take his army back through the Pass of Kitos, its tail between its legs. Further fighting could turn Trawn's defeat into a rout. It would also involve gambling Draad's whole army. That meant eight thousand warriors plus all the civilians who'd done their work so well today but who would certainly be doomed if the battle turned violently and suddenly against Draad.

No, the battle would go on. He would gamble. Trawn's army might not march away if he left it alone. Desgo had much more to avenge now than simply an arrow in his behind, and all his men doubtless had comrades to avenge. The enemy might stay, and then there would be many thousands of dead in Draad's villages and camps. In the end there would be another battle, perhaps under less favorable circumstances.

Even if Trawn's army went away now, it might return soon. Trawn's warriors had suffered, but they had not been beaten and smashed and driven. They had not taken a defeat that would keep them on the other side of the Mountains of Hoga for two generations. Blade wanted to pound them that badly. He sensed that every man in the army around him wanted the same thing. There were too many years of blood and hatred meeting on this field in this battle to let him call the battle off now.

Blade rose in his stirrups and signaled to the trumpeters. The two thousand warriors lined up in columns on each side of him saw the signal and a ripple of tension went up and down both columns. Then the trumpeters sounded, and the attack rolled forward. Beside Blade rode Neena, and around the two of them ten more warriors on captured meytans.

Those meytans were one more of Blade's tricks. They were slow to breed, slow to mature, hard to keep alive, and therefore rare and expensive. There were less than a thousand of them in all of Trawn, and most of those were used for ceremonial purposes rather than trained for war. Desgo must have put in a great deal of time and effort to get the forty or so he'd brought on this campaign with him.

So Trawn had no cavalry and no tradition of fighting on horseback. That should mean they also had no tradition of fighting against men on horseback. In theory, they should be completely unable to defend themselves against any sort of cavalry charge.

So completely, that a charge with only a dozen meytans could crack their line? That was a good question. It was also one that would be answered in about two more minutes.

The attacking columns started their advance at a walk. The leaders of the columns pushed through the civilians. They broke into a trot and pushed through the front line, a thin screen of warriors concealing the civilians. As they reached the open, the leaders sounded their war cries and broke into a dead run.

At the same moment Blade and his little band of cavalry dug in their spurs. The warriors who'd been running in front of the meytans dashed to either side. Straight in front of him Blade saw the enemy's line. He dug his spurs in still deeper and the meytan surged forward, its six legs rapidly working up to a pounding gallop.

Blade's mouth was dry with tension. It would not take long to reach the enemy line. It would take long enough for Trawn's archers to slaughter him and Neena and the men riding with them if they stood their ground and took careful aim.

The seconds went by, with war cries and the thunder of hooves deafening in Blade's ears. He bent low against the meytan's neck, at any moment expecting to hear the whistle of arrows and feel the red-hot stab of them in his flesh.

Then suddenly the line of warriors facing him shivered, writhed, and began to disintegrate. Blade sat up in his saddle with a roar of triumph and drew his sword as his meytan thundered down at the space where the enemy line had been.

He'd been right. Against even the smallest cavalry charge Trawn's warriors could think of nothing but fleeing. Fifty yards of Trawn's line was gone as completely as if Blade had dropped a salvo of shells on it. Some of the warriors ran to either side, joining their comrades. Others were not worrying about comrades, battle, honor, or anything else. They were running like rabbits, hurling down weapons as they ran, heading west toward the Pass of Kitos. Blade gave another triumphant roar as he saw that, and heard his cry echoed by Neena.

Then the two columns of running warriors smashed into the shaken men on either side of the gap torn by the cavalry. Suddenly those men found themselves holding down flanks that hadn't existed ten seconds before, holding them against a swarm of enemy warriors who screamed and shrieked, swinging axes and thrusting with spears like madmen.

The extreme right flank of Desgo's army was completely cut off by Blade's attack. The warriors there stood their ground for as much as a minute, until they realized their situation. Then they crumbled away, half of them fleeing without striking a blow, nearly all of them heading west out of the battle. The warriors of Draad saw their enemies in flight and turned to join their comrades on the right.

There stood most of Desgo's army, and for the moment it was stronger and not as badly shaken. Some men had fled, others had died surrounded by overwhelming numbers, but many had struggled back to join their comrades. Slowly Desgo's battle line folded back on itself, and the

177

thin flank facing Blade's men grew into a thick mass of warriors fighting for their lives.

This was something Blade had hoped he wouldn't see. But he'd made plans to meet it and now he put them into action. More trumpets, and the rest of Draad's warriors swarmed forward, leaping up from behind the dead stolofs where they'd been taking cover. The archers came on firing as they ran, sending a deadly close-range fire into Trawn's ranks. The other warriors came on, brandishing swords and iron-tipped spears they'd snatched up from the dead on the ground. All of them stormed forward with yells and screams like a host of fiends bursting out of the earth. They crashed into the rest of Trawn's battle line with the impact of five thousand running men who will not be stopped by anything except death. With that impact they broke their enemy.

Blade saw it as he rode up and down on the left flank of the battle. He and the cavalry were not trying to ride into the fighting. He hadn't been able to teach anyone except Neena how to fight from the back of a meytan. The rest of the cavalrymen had already dismounted, their job as a battering ram done, and joined the fighting on foot.

Neena shouted first as she saw Trawn's army starting to crumble, and Blade echoed her. Then Neena gave a shout of a very different sort, and Blade spun around in the saddle to see Lord Desgo charging down on them. There was foam on the lips of his meytan, and Blade wasn't quite sure that there wasn't foam on Lord Desgo's own lips.

Lord Desgo saw his defeated and crumbling army, the head of his meytan, the mountains on one side and the forests on the other. He saw all of them through a red haze of fury. He saw only one thing in all the world clearly, and that was Prince Blade. The gods had sent him and Trawn defeat. This he knew. But surely in his last moments they would not also deny him vengeance against Blade and Neena?

He drew his sword, threw back his head, and let a terrible scream tear up from deep inside him. There was

178

rage and hatred and fear and despair in that scream, a knowledge of his own death, and the desperate hope that he would be able to take the man who had destroyed him down into death along with him.

Neena's meytan bolted at Lord Desgo's scream. It angled sharply away to the right, toward the enemy's flank. Blade swore as he realized the runaway animal was going to take Neena right down behind Trawn's battle line. The archers would have an easy target, and even the spearmen would be—

Neena stood up in her stirrups. With the skill of a circus rider she swung from the stirrups up into the saddle, balancing there with inhuman ease and grace. Then she leaped high, tumbling head over heels, soaring toward the enemy line, soaring over it. She twisted in midair to avoid the jutting spears, then landed in an open space only a few feet from Draad's line. Before a single warrior of Trawn could lift a finger against her, she plunged into the safety of Draad's ranks. They folded themselves around their princess, and she vanished from Blade's sight.

A moment later he had problems of his own. Blade and Lord Desgo had both been staring at Neena's fantastic leap so hard that they completely forgot about each other. Their meytans nearly crashed head-on into each other. They pulled them aside with feet to spare and charged past each other.

As he pulled his meytan around, Blade saw Lord Desgo doing the same. For a moment he wondered what to do next. He had no weapon with enough reach to match Lord Desgo's two-handed sword. But he had a captured Trawn short sword, he knew how to throw it, and Lord Desgo wore no armor. Blade drew the sword and hefted it by the tip as he and Lord Desgo charged past each other again. Then they were coming back around, into a third charge, with Desgo heading straight toward the Mountains of Hoga. Blade's arm whipped up and out, and the short sword sank into Desgo's belly just below his rib cage.

He screamed, as much in surprise as in pain, and reeled

179

in his saddle. Then he toppled to one side, sliding toward the ground. He did not fall all the way. One foot caught in a stirrup. As the panic-stricken meytan galloped away, Lord Desgo went with it, dragged along the ground and bounced into the air by every rough spot he went over. His face was already a pulped, bloody mask as Blade lost sight of him.

Lord Desgo's eyes must have closed for good long before his army finally broke and ran from the field. The gods had not spared him much, but they did spare him that.

The army of Draad never *did* find out what its opponents' trumpets sounded like in defeat. All of Trawn's trumpeters were either dead or too busy running for their lives to have any breath to spare for their music.

Chapter 28

It was the evening of the day of the battle. Blade, King Embor, Neena, and the High Kaireen were sitting in a dark and drafty hut not far from the battlefield. A small fire burned in the center of the floor, producing nearly as much smoke as light.

It produced enough light to show an enormous emerald flashing on Neena's left hand. Her betrothal ring was finished at last, delivered by messenger only an hour after the battle.

The same firelight showed the ruby ring once more on Blade's hand. He was not as delighted as Neena, but it was certainly a load off his mind. His time in this dimension must be drawing toward a close. When he was snatched back to Home Dimension, he wanted to be wearing that ring. It was the first object ever to pass with him into Dimension X, and that made it too important to leave with anyone, for any reason.

King Embor was talking.

"—not as happy as I might be. We have the bodies of

ten thousand of Trawn's warriors, with all their weapons and gear. We have the camp, with everything and everyone in it. We have slain most of Trawn's trained stolofs, and also Lord Desgo himself. Yet is this enough? Half of the enemy's warriors have escaped us."

Neena shook her head. "They have escaped us here, on the battlefield, today. That does not mean they will find a safe way home. The Pass of Kitos is held against them, and the mountain people will also do their part. I doubt if more than half the survivors will get through the pass. Half of those will die in the forests, of hunger and thirst, snakes and falls, drowning and the arrows of the mountain people who will still be following them. Those who return to Trawn will be starved, sick, and wearing nothing but their breech clouts, if that much. I think we have taught Draad a lesson that they will not forget in our time or in our children's, at least."

The High Kaireen nodded. "I agree with the princess. Also, we have another weapon against them, one my people have discovered while searching the camp." He held out a thick wad of parchment scrolls tied up with deerskin thongs.

"Lord Desgo apparently had hopes of making himself a ruler of Draad after he smashed our camp. Then he would use our wealth to win friends among the nobles of Trawn, and in the end lead them against Furzun and sit upon the throne of Trawn himself."

"I'm not surprised," said Blade. "His ambitions stuck out all over him."

"He certainly was ambitious," said the High Kaireen. His smile broadened. "He also was not very wise. He wrote many letters to those he hoped would some day be his firm allies, and received many replies. Here they are." He dropped the scrolls on the floor.

"I too would say that he was not wise," said Embor. "But what does this mean for us?"

Blade grinned. "It means a great deal. Have you thought what may happen in Trawn if we get these letters into King Furzun's hands?"

Neena gave a whoop of delight. "He will be too busy

tracking down all of Desgo's friends and taking off their heads to think about anything else. There will be complete chaos in Trawn for at least a year, and much bitterness after that."

"Assuming that one of those nobles doesn't decide to try getting the king first," added Blade. *"Then* there will be civil war in Trawn, and chaos for ten years instead of one."

King Embor nodded. "All this is very good, but how are we to get the letters into Furzun's hands?"

"I think we should—" began the High Kaireen, but Neena held up a hand to stop him.

"If you two wish to sit up all night planning how to confound Trawn even further, well and good. Blade and I will not be needed. I think we can leave, can we not, father?"

Embor sighed and smiled wearily. "You can, daughter. But first I have something for your husband." He reached into a bag beside him and drew out a small sack of fine white deerskin with a copper and gold fastening. He handed it to Blade.

"Open it, my son."

Blade opened it. A dozen emeralds, from the size of a baby's fist on down to the size of marbles, flashed fire back at him. Between exhaustion and gratitude, he found himself unable to say anything for a moment. Then all he could say was, "Thank you, my Lord," before Neena grabbed his hand and practically dragged him out of the hut.

Outside in the cool night air Blade took several deep breaths and felt his head become clearer. He also felt Neena lean against him, running her hands over his body in a way that could have only one meaning.

"Neena, are you never satisfied?"

"It has been a long time since we last joined, my husband."

"It has only been since last night, wife."

"That is a long time, when we have spent a day so full of danger that each minute seemed like an hour. Come

182

with me, and let us rejoice together that we have won and that both of us are alive to celebrate it."

Blade could not argue with those sentiments. He followed Neena toward their own hut without another word.

They undressed in the darkness and lay down beside each other on the straw pallet that was all the bedding. After the day's fighting, it seemed as comfortable to both of them as a feather mattress. Neena's lips moved toward Blade's, pressing themselves down warmly and eagerly. Her hands explored his body, stroking their way down into his groin, as his hands crept up her graceful curves to her breasts.

They joined, and a glorious flame seemed to be burning deep inside Blade. It was in his groin, in all his limbs, in his head—

His head! A second before the pain in his head became agonizing instead of glorious, Blade knew what was happening. He was going Home, gripped by the computer, about to be snatched away from Gleor—and from Neena.

She had noticed that something was wrong. She cried out, not in pleasure but in fear of the totally unknown and of danger to him. The pain in Blade's head blazed higher, and it seemed to him that the whole dark hut was being flooded with light. He saw Neena's wide-eyed face inches from him, and he saw the bag of emeralds lying on the floor beside the pallet. One hand stabbed out frantically and clutched the bag.

Then in another moment the whole hut and the ground under it seemed to tilt violently on end. Suddenly the floor was vertical. Blade was falling, falling away from Neena, falling down through the wall that had suddenly become a floor, falling down into nothing. The air whistled past him as he fell and he began to tumble head over heels. He tumbled faster and faster, until he was spinning downward like a pinwheel. The blood began to pool in his head and the world around him began to turn red—

—until between one second and the next the whirling and the fall and the redness all came to an end. He was sitting in the chair in the computer room below the Tower of London. On his finger glinted the ruby ring; in his

183

hand was the bag of emeralds. On the faces of J and Lord Leighton was relief, and as they stared at the ruby ring, there was also delight and even triumph.

Chapter 29

Lord Leighton sat in a chair in his study and looked at his desk. On his desk was a small box filled with cotton wool. On the cotton wool sat Richard Blade's ruby ring. It did not look like much—it never had. But Leighton was happier to see it there than he would have been to see the crown jewels of England in the same place, let alone the sack of emeralds that *did* sit on the polished wood beside the little box!

That ring was the first object in the whole world—other than Richard Blade himself, of course—to make the round trip into Dimension X and back again. It could now be said that it was *not* impossible for Blade to go into Dimension X with something other than his bare hands, his bare skin, and his own wits. J would be delighted at that—in fact, he already was.

Lord Leighton was also happy enough. But he would have been even happier if the ring hadn't represented such a *theoretical* solution to the problem of equipping Blade for his trips into Dimension X. And theoretical solutions had a way of dissolving like mist in the sunlight when you started looking at them more closely.

Besides, even if they were on the right track, they were still a long way from a reliable solution. Leighton remembered the words of his chemistry instructor at Oxford, in those golden days even before World War I. "Leighton," the man had said, "you will find in time that every theoretical solution generates at least ten practical problems on the way."

The instructor was long dead—killed on the Somme in 1916, as a matter of fact—but during all those years Leighton had never found anything to disprove those words. They had always been true, and probably always would be, not only for the rest of Leighton's own life but for as long as there was such a thing as experimental science in the world!

Consider what they faced with this ring. Was the secret of its traveling into Dimension X in its composition—its alloying, perhaps?

Perhaps. But how to find out the exact formula, in that case? The jeweler who'd made the ring was long gone, and unfortunately so were all the relevant records, destroyed when his shop was blitzed in 1941.

Take a sample from the ring? That could be done, but there wasn't much to it. Taking that sample could destroy the ring. Certainly it would alter it. That would not only be destroying or damaging their only specimen, it would be destroying some of Richard Blade's personal property. Leighton was normally rather ruthless about minor bits of other people's property, although it was *not* true that he would have boiled his own mother in oil to ensure meaningful results for an experiment. He made an exception for Richard Blade, however.

Suppose it was not some physical property of the ring that was involved? Suppose Blade's "guess" turned out to make sense after all, that there *was* some paranormal affinity between a man and something that had been in his possession for as long as the ring?

Leighton didn't know. He *did* know that he wouldn't get much in the way of useful data by turning the matter over to the existing staff of project psychologists. They would dismiss any notion of paranormal phenomena as arrant, mystical nonsense, unworthy of serious consideration.

Leighton didn't hold that view. He was not a mystic, he was merely a determined nonbeliever in the arrogant, cocksure view of regular psychologists on matters paranormal. He did not consider that arrogance a proper scientific attitude, and he made no secret of his opinion.

That was all very well and good, but it still meant that he would have to go outside the project for anyone to research the paranormal possibilities in this situation.

That would in turn mean more security clearances to be handled, and more work for J—who was already overburdened with work. He was still trying to get Scotland Yard off the trail of the "mystery man" of the train wreck—and without getting the Prime Minister involved, a solution which would cause more problems than it solved!

Besides, the security aspects of hiring paranormal researchers would be even more ticklish than usual. The Russians were decades ahead of the West in everything having to do with the paranormal. They placed great importance on research in the area and financed and staffed their projects accordingly.

Logically, that also meant they put a lot of time into keeping tabs on what paranormal researchers in the West were doing—if anything. When the Russians decided to keep tabs on something abroad, they could be very thorough and were almost always fairly ruthless. It could be a ticklish problem, finding a reliable paranormal researcher *and* hiring him under circumstances that would not come to the attention of the KGB. Lord Leighton had already tackled one confrontation with the KGB, when Katerina Shumilova tried to sabotage the computer. She had ended up in Dimension X for her pains, and that was the end of her. Next time the solution might not come so easily, and frankly Leighton would be much happier if there *were* no "next time" at all. But on still another hand, he couldn't let the risk of tangling with the Russians scare him off from a possibly important line of research, otherwise—

Leighton laughed out loud and carefully shifted his mind away from the project. Sitting here working himself into a mild stew over the project's murky future was an exercise in futility. It would solve none of the problems, and it might end up costing him even those few hours of sleep that he still needed. It was time for a nightcap, then bed.

Leighton rose, closed the box on the ring, put it in his pocket, turned off the lights, and went out of the room.